Eça de Queiroz

The Mandarin and Other Stories

Translated and with an introduction by
Margaret Jull Costa

Dedalus

CALOUSTE
GULBENKIAN
FOUNDATION

Dedalus would like to thank the Calouste Gulbenkian Foundation for its support in producing this book.

Published in the UK by Dedalus Limited
24–26, St Judith's Lane, Sawtry, Cambs, PE28 5XE
email: info@dedalusbooks.com
www.dedalusbooks.com

ISBN 978 1 903517 80 2

Dedalus is distributed in the USA by SCB Distributors,
15608 South New Century Drive, Gardena, CA 90248
email: info@scbdistributors.com   web site: www.scbdistributors.com

Dedalus is distributed in Australia by Peribo Pty Ltd.
58, Beaumont Road, Mount Kuring-gai N.S.W. 2080
email: info@peribo.com.au

Dedalus is distributed in Canada by Disticor Direct-Book Division
695, Westney Road South, Suite 14, Ajax, Ontario, LI6 6M9
email: ndalton@disticor.com   web site: www.disticordirect.com

Publishing History
The Mandarin and 'José Matías' were first published by Dedalus in 1993.
Revised and republished with the addition of 'The Idiosyncrasies of a Young Blonde Woman' and 'The Hanged Man' in 2009.
First published in Portugal in 1880, 1897, 1873 and 1895.

Translation and Introduction copyright © Margaret Jull Costa 1993 and 2009

The right of Margaret Jull Costa to be indentified as the translator of this work has been asserted by her in accordance with the Copyright, Designs and Patent Act, 1988

Printed in Finland by WS. Bookwell
Typeset by RefineCatch Limited, Bungay, Suffolk

A C.I.P. listing for this book is available on request.

THE TRANSLATOR

Margaret Jull Costa has translated many novels and short stories by Portuguese and Spanish writers, among them Fernando Pessoa, Mário de Sá-Carneiro, José Saramago, Ramón del Valle-Inclán, Javier Marías and Bernardo Atxaga.

Her work has brought her various prizes, the most recent being the 2008 PEN/Book-of-the-Month Prize and the 2008 Oxford Weidenfeld Award for her translation of Eça de Queiroz's masterpiece *The Maias*.

Portuguese Literature from Dedalus

CALOUSTE
GULBENKIAN
FOUNDATION

Dedalus, as part of its Europe 1992–2012 programme, with the assistance of the Portuguese Book Institute, the Camões Institute in Lisbon and the Calouste Gulbenkian Foundation, has embarked on a series of new translations by Margaret Jull Costa of some of the major classics of Portuguese Literature.

Titles so far published:

The City and the Mountains – Eça de Queiroz
Cousin Bazilio – Eça de Queiroz
The Crime of Father Amaro – Eça de Queiroz
The Maias - Eça de Queiroz
The Mandarin and Other Stories - Eça de Queiroz
The Relic – Eça de Queiroz
The Tragedy of the Street of Flowers - Eça de Queiroz
Lúcio's Confession – Mário de Sá-Carneiro
The Great Shadow and Other Stories – Mário de Sá-Carneiro
The Dedalus Book of Portuguese Fantasy – Editors: Eugénio Lisboa and Helder Macedo

Forthcoming titles include:

Alves & Co and Other Stories - Eça de Queiroz
The Illustrious House of Ramires - Eça de Queiroz

Contents

INTRODUCTION

José Maria de Eça de Queiroz was born on 25th November 1845 in the small town of Póvoa de Varzim in the north of Portugal. His mother was nineteen and unmarried. Only the name of his father appears on the birth certificate. Following the birth, his mother returned immediately to her respectable family in Viana do Castelo, and Eça was left with his wetnurse, who looked after him for six years until her death. Although his parents did marry – when Eça was four – and went on to have six more children, Eça did not live with them until he was twenty-one, living instead either with his grandparents or at boarding school in Oporto, where he spent the holidays with an aunt. His father only officially acknowledged Eça as his son when the latter was forty. He did, however, pay for his son's studies at boarding school and at Coimbra University, where Eça studied Law, and was always supportive of his writing ambitions. After working as the editor and sole contributor on a provincial newspaper in Évora, Eça made a trip to the Middle East with his friend and future brother-in-law, Luís de Resende. Then, in order to launch himself on a diplomatic career, he worked for six months in Leiria, a provincial town north of Lisbon, as a municipal administrator before being appointed consul in Havana (1872–74), Newcastle-upon-Tyne (1874–79) and Bristol (1879–88). In 1886, he married Emília de Castro with whom he had four children. His last consular posting was to Paris in 1888, and he served there until his death in 1900 at the age of only 54. He had been suffering for years with gastric problems, which doctors diagnosed as gastro-intestinal malaria. He went to Switzerland in search of treatment, but when his health continued to decline, he decided to return home. He arrived in Paris on 13th August and died on the 16th. His wish to be buried beside his grandfather in the cemetery at Oliveirinha was ignored, and he was laid to rest instead in his wife's family vault in Alto de São João.

He began writing stories and essays as a young man and became involved with a group of intellectuals known as the Generation of 1870, who were committed to reforms in society and in the arts. During his lifetime, he published five novels and one novella: *The Mystery of the Sintra Road* (in collaboration with Ramalho Ortigão: 1870), *The Crime of Father Amaro* (3 versions: 1875, 1876, 1880), *Cousin Bazilio* (1878), *The Mandarin* (1880), *The Relic* (1887) and *The Maias* (1888). His other works were published posthumously: *The City and the Mountains, The Illustrious House of Ramires, To the Capital, Alves & Co., The Letters of Fradique Mendes, The Count of Abranhos* and *The Tragedy of the Street of Flowers*.

★ ★ ★

Eça wrote *The Mandarin* in 1880 in order to keep a promise to a friend, Lourenço Malheiro, the editor of the *Diário de Portugal*. He had earlier agreed that the newspaper would serialise *The Maias*. When the time came, however, *The Maias* was still unfinished (indeed it was only published in 1888), and so, while he was on holiday in Angers, he began to write *The Mandarin*, which the *Diário* duly serialised in eleven episodes.

Now, depending on which dictionary you consult, the French expression '*tuer le mandarin*' ['to kill the mandarin'] means either to commit some evil act in the hope that no one will ever find out, or to harm someone whom you know you will never meet in order to gain some personal advantage and in the certain knowledge that you will never be punished. The expression is said to have its origins in the 'mandarin paradox', first formulated by Chateaubriand in 1802 in *Génie du christianisme* and later taken up by other French writers. *The Mandarin* is based on this paradox, which Eça restates thus:

> In the depths of China there lives a mandarin who is richer than any king spoken of in fable or in history. You know nothing about him, not his name, his face or the silks

10

that he wears. In order for you to inherit his limitless wealth, all you have to do is to ring the bell placed on a book by your side. In that remote corner of Mongolia, he will utter a single sigh. He will then be a corpse, and at your feet you will see gold beyond the dreams of avarice. Mortal reader, will you ring the bell?

Needless to say, Teodoro – a lowly government clerk with dreams of a more glamorous lifestyle – rings the bell and, ultimately, pays the price for his indifference and greed. What, in other less skilful hands, might become heavily moral, is delivered by Eça with a wonderful lightness of touch, and Teodoro, or, rather, his newly acquired wealth, becomes a kind of touchstone by which others are judged; almost all are found wanting.

In a lecture given in 1871 in Lisbon, Eça, a great admirer of Flaubert's work, spoke of realism as the only way forward for literature. Nine years later, when he wrote *The Mandarin*, he found himself in the curious position of being criticised for abandoning the realist aesthetic in favour of fantasy. Eça responded to this criticism in an introduction he wrote for the French edition, saying, doubtless tongue in cheek:

. . . it is precisely because this book belongs to the realm of dreams rather than reality, because it is invented and not the fruit of observation, that it . . . more faithfully embodies the natural, spontaneous impulse of the Portuguese spirit.

The truth is that Eça was far too interesting an author to be pigeonholed as a realist or a naturalist, a writer of fantasies, a Romantic or whatever. It becomes clear from *The Mandarin* onwards that Eça rejected all such labels, and that while the books he wrote thereafter sometimes include fantastical elements – for example, *The Relic, The City and the Mountains, The Illustrious House of Ramires* – or resort to those favourite Romantic plot devices, fate and coincidence – as in *The Maias* and *The Tragedy of the Street of Flowers* – or could be described as social satire – such as *To the Capital, The Count of Abranhos* –

none can ever be neatly labelled as purely and simply fantasy, Romance or satire.

The Mandarin is undoubtedly a fantasy, but it is set in a very recognisable Lisbon, and when Teodoro arrives in China, while the clothes and shops may be exotic, and the landscape wilder and bleaker, the mores are little different from those prevalent in nineteenth-century Portugal. Like all the best fantasies, *The Mandarin* ultimately has its feet firmly in reality.

* * *

The other three stories in this collection – the first written more than twenty years before the others – reveal Eça in all his literary diversity.

Eça wrote 'The Idiosyncrasies of a Young Blonde Woman' in 1873, in Cuba, where he had his first diplomatic posting (an otherwise fallow period in his writing career). It was his first largely realist story and takes a deliberately anti-Romantic stance. A sceptical narrator tells us a tale told to him by a man, Macário, whom he met at an inn. Macário's whole life has been blighted by his love for pretty, blonde, vacuous Luísa. In the blindness of his love for her – or is it his innocence of the ways of the world? – he fails to ask certain vital questions. What is her real position in society? Is her voluptuous and very dark-haired mother really her mother? Who and where is her father? How do they manage to live? When his uncle (his sole relative *and* his employer) refuses to support him in his desire to marry her, Macário puts this down to meanness of spirit, rather than wondering if perhaps his uncle knows something he does not. In the end, his romantic attachment to Luísa dies from a severe dose of reality.

'The Hanged Man', written in 1895, is based on a sermon given by the Jesuit Father António Vieira, who was considered to be one of the greatest orators of the seventeenth century. Eça's version follows Vieira's story very closely, but Eça breathes warm humanity into what was originally a purely moral tale. He puts us inside the innocent wife's mind as she ponders the consequences of her jealous husband's foolish actions, and endows the hanged man with impeccable

12

manners and the ability to savour the pleasure of being able to move freely again, as he runs alongside Don Ruy and his horse. 'How good it is to run again!' he mutters to himself.

'José Matías', written in 1897, is one of Eça's most famous stories, in which he takes a literary idea – Romantic love – to its fantastical and logical extreme. The unnamed narrator is a Hegelian philosopher on his way to José Matías' funeral. He recounts to an unnamed silent listener the strange and tragic life of José and his love for Elisa. He sees their relationship as an example of the dialectic between spirit and flesh, between idealism and materialism, and cannot help but feel a grudging admiration for José's stubborn determination to love Elisa on his own terms, with a love that will not fit comfortably into any philosophy and that sets up a further and perhaps more troubling dialectic, between absurdity and nobility of heart.

All three stories are accounts of one man's obsession with a woman, a theme that runs through much of Eça's work, and while Eça sees that such an obsession can be a driving force that reveals unexpected strengths and talents – as is the case here with Macário in 'Idiosyncrasies' – he never sees it as an engine that will propel the obsessed person towards happiness or fulfilment. Such obsessive love is based on fantasy, not reality. The narrator of 'José Matías' suspects that José simply

> . . . had a horror of the material aspects of marriage: the slippers, the touch of clammy morning skin, the six long months of enormous swelling belly, the children screaming in their wet beds . . . [and] could never imagine that slippers and dirty nappies are things of great beauty in a house filled by sunlight and love.

José Matías' love is too pure to contemplate the essentially unromantic nature of married life and children; Macário's romantic love for Luísa blinds him to the true nature of her and of her life; the husband in 'The Hanged Man', eaten up by jealousy and insecurity, is unable to believe in his young wife's innocence.

Even in his earlier, more realist novels, Eça often made imaginative use of dreams as a way of letting fantasy inform reality, and it seems to me that in his subsequent works, he uses fantasy as a means of illuminating reality, never as an escape from it, recognising perhaps that fantasy – in the shape of dreams, stories and imagination – is vital to all human beings and that maintaining a balance between fantasy and reality is essential to our sanity. Thus the characters and the world described in Eça's so-called fantasies are as convincing and as real as those in his so-called realist works. He was, in short, far too intelligent, too humane and imaginative a writer to submit to the straitjacket of any one literary school.

THE MANDARIN

Prologue

Friend no. 1 (sitting on a terrace beneath some trees, by the sea, sipping brandy and soda)

My friend, let us succumb to this heavy summer heat that blunts the cutting edge of wisdom and rest a while from the harsh study of human Reality. Let us depart instead for the fields of Dreams and wander those blue, romantic hills where stands the abandoned tower of the Supernatural, where cool mosses clothe the ruins of Idealism. Let us, in short, indulge in a little fantasy!

Friend no. 2

But let us do so soberly and temperately, my friend! And, as in the wise and amiable allegories of the Renaissance, let us add just a pinch of Morality.

(From an unpublished play)

1

My name is Teodoro and I was once a scribe at the Ministry for Internal Affairs and Education.

At the time, I lived at 106 Travessa da Conceição in a guest-house run by the splendid Dona Augusta, the widow of Major Marques. I had two fellow lodgers: Cabrita, who was as thin and yellow as a funeral candle and worked as a clerk on the city council, and the vigorous, exuberant Lieutenant Couceiro, who played the guitar extremely well.

My existence was one of sweet regularity. During the week I would sit down at my office desk, put on my silk oversleeves and set to work covering sheets of official notepaper in my exquisite italic script, always using the same glib phrases: *Esteemed Sir, I have the honour to inform you . . ., I have the pleasure of sending Your Honour . . ., Illustrious Sir . . .*

On Sundays I rested. Installed on the sofa in the dining room, my pipe clenched between my teeth, I would gaze admiringly at Dona Augusta whose custom it was, on holy days, to massage away Lieutenant Couceiro's dandruff with the judicious application of eggwhite. That was always a delightful time of day, especially in summer: the hot breath of noon would waft in through the half-open windows along with the distant ringing of the bells of Conceição Nova and the cooing of doves on the verandah whilst, inside, the mono-tonous drone of flies hovered above the old cambric cloth (formerly Madame Marques' wedding veil) draped over the sideboard to protect the plates of cherries. The lieutenant, wrapped in a sheet like an idol in a cloak, would drift slowly off to sleep beneath the gentle friction of Dona Augusta's loving hands and she, sticking out one plump, white little finger, would plough through the Lieutenant's thinning but lustrous hair with a fine-toothed comb . . . In the emotion of the moment I would exclaim to the charming lady:

'Ah, Dona Augusta, what an angel you are!'

She would laugh and call me 'Pipsqueak' and I would smile, not in the least offended. In fact that was the name the whole house knew me by. Why? Because I was skinny, always took care to enter a room right foot first, trembled at the mere sight of a mouse, kept a lithograph of Our Lady of Sorrows that had once belonged to Mama above my bed and had a pronounced stoop. The stoop, alas, was the consequence of the many times I had bent my back before the dons at University, retreating from them like a startled magpie, and before the directors-general at work, in whose presence I practically touched my forehead to the ground. Indeed, such an attitude is only proper in a young graduate, the very basis of order in a well-organized state and, besides, it guaranteed me my Sunday peace, an adequate supply of clean linen and twenty *mil-réis* a month.

I cannot deny, however, that at the time, as Madame Marques and the jovial Lieutenant Couceiro both had the wit to acknowledge, I did harbour certain ambitions. I do not mean that there stirred in my breast any heroic desire to rule from some lofty throne over vast hordes of people nor that my mad soul longed to ride through the Baixa in a company carriage, with a lackey trotting behind me. No, what consumed me was the desire to partake of champagne suppers at the Hotel Central, to clasp the delicate hands of a viscountess in mine and, at least twice a week, to fall asleep in dumb ecstasy on the cool breast of some Venus. Oh, you young men making your happy way to the opera house, in your expensive overcoats and gleaming white cravats! Oh, you carriages crammed with lovely Andalusian women, rattling elegantly off to see a bullfight – how I sighed for you! For then, the certain knowledge that my measly twenty *mil-réis* a month and my pipsqueak looks excluded me for ever from such social pleasures would pierce my heart like an arrow which, shot into the trunk of a tree, remained there for a long time afterwards, poised and quivering!

But for all that, I never thought of myself gloomily as a 'pariah'. The humble life has its compensatory pleasures:

opening up that day's *Diário de Notícias* on a bright, sunny morning, with a napkin round your neck and a grilled steak on the plate before you; savouring the sweet idyll of summer evenings spent sitting on the public benches in the park; or listening to the armchair politicians running down the country as you sip your coffee at night in the Café Martinho . . . I never much suffered from unhappiness; I lacked the necessary imagination. I did not torment myself by prowling longingly about the fringes of fictitious paradises that emanated only from my own eager heart like clouds of mist rising from a lake. I did not gaze up at the luminous stars and sigh for a love like Romeo's or for the social success of a Camors. Being a practical sort of person, I aspired only to what was reasonable, tangible, to what others like myself had already attained, to what a graduate might realistically hope to achieve. And I became resigned to my fate, like someone at a *table d'hôte* meal chewing patiently on a mouthful of dry bread while he waits for them to serve up a delicious *charlotte russe*. Happiness would arrive one day and to hasten its arrival I did everything that a good Portuguese and a constitutionalist could do: I prayed every night to Our Lady of Sorrows and bought lottery tickets, the cheapest available.

In the meantime, I did my best to amuse myself. And since the convolutions of my brain did not equip me to write poetry, which was what so many of my colleagues did to avenge themselves on the tedium of their profession, and since my salary, once I'd paid the rent and bought my cigarettes, was insufficient to accommodate any vice, I had acquired the discreet habit of scouring the local flea market for incomplete sets of old books and at night in my room I would gorge myself on those curious texts. They always bore portentous titles: *The Ship of Innocence, The Miraculous Mirror, The Despair of the Disinherited* . . . The antiquated typeface, the yellowing, worm-eaten paper, the sombre, monkish binding, the little green ribbon marking one's place – all that enchanted me! The ingenuous words set down in large clumsy print bathed my whole being in a kind of serenity, the sort of penetrating peace one might feel at the end of a quiet afternoon, standing

19

by a ruined monastery wall at the bottom of a valley, listening to the sad babble of a stream.

One night, years ago now, I had begun reading a chapter in one of those ancient folios entitled 'The Abyss of Souls' and I was just drifting off into a pleasant state of drowsiness when one particular passage suddenly stood out from the dull, neutral tone of the rest of the page, like a new gold medal gleaming against a dark carpet. I give below the exact words:

In the depths of China there lives a mandarin who is richer than any king spoken of in fable or in history. You know nothing about him, not his name, his face or the silks that he wears. In order for you to inherit his limitless wealth, all you have to do is to ring the bell placed on a book by your side. In that remote corner of Mongolia, he will utter a single sigh. He will then be a corpse and at your feet you will see gold beyond the dreams of avarice. Mortal reader, will you ring the bell?

Startled, I stared down at the open page. That question: Mortal reader, will you ring the bell? struck me as playful, even absurd and yet it troubled me terribly. I wanted to read on but the lines on the page slipped away from me like frightened snakes and, in the emptiness they left behind, pale as parchment, there remained only that strange demand, gleaming blackly up at me: Will you ring the bell?

Had the book been some straightforward tome published in a yellow binding by Michel-Lévy, I would have simply closed it there and then and put an end to such febrile imaginings. I was not, after all, lost in a forest in some German ballad; indeed from my balcony I could see the belts of the policemen on patrol glinting white in the gaslight. But a kind of magic seemed to emanate from that lugubrious book. Every letter took on the disquieting form of symbols in the ancient kabbala, each possessed of prophetic qualities: the commas formed petulant curves like the tails of demons glimpsed in the pale moonlight; in that final question mark I saw the fearful hook with which the Tempter fishes for those souls who fall asleep without first taking refuge in the inviolable citadel of Prayer! Some supernatural power took hold of me, dragged me slowly away from reality, away from reason, and in my spirit two visions began to take shape – on the one hand I imagined a decrepit old mandarin, far off in a Chinese pavilion, dying painlessly at the tinkle of a bell; on the other I saw a mountain of gold glittering at my feet! So real were these visions that I could actually see the slanted eyes of that noble old personage grow dim, as if slowly covered over by a fine layer of dust, and I could hear the light clink of coins one against the other. And sitting absolutely still, my skin prickling, I fixed my burning eyes on the bell perched peaceably beside me on a French dictionary, just as the marvellous book had both foreseen and described . . .

It was then, from the other side of my bedside table, that an insinuating, metallic voice spoke to me out of the silence:

'Come on, Teodoro, my friend, reach out your hand, ring the bell, be a man!'

The green shade on the candle cast a shadow round about. Trembling, I picked the candle up. Seated calmly before me, I saw a bulky figure, all dressed in black, a tall hat on his head and his two hands encased in black gloves resting gravely on the handle of an umbrella. There was nothing fantastic about him. He seemed so contemporary, so ordinary, so middle class; he could have been a fellow scribe at the ministry . . .

His originality lay entirely in the strong, hard lines of his beardless face. His sharp nose, formidably aquiline, had all the rapacity of an eagle's beak; the line of his lips was so firm as to seem cast in bronze; his eyes, when they looked at me, were like two flares sent up from amongst the swarthy brambles of his eyebrows that met above his nose; his face was deathly pale, but here and there his skin was threaded with red veins like old Phoenician marble.

It suddenly occurred to me that the person sitting before me must be the Devil, but my reason immediately rebelled against such imaginings. I have never believed in the Devil, just as I have never believed in God. I never said as much out loud or wrote about it in the newspapers, not wishing to annoy the powers-that-be, whose duty it is to preserve public respect for such entities. But the idea that these two characters, old as Matter itself, actually exist like good-natured rivals playing amiable pranks on each other – one in the guise of old Jove, in a white beard and blue tunic, inhabiting the luminous heights, where he is surrounded by a court more complicated than Louis XIV's, and the other, soot-besmirched and sly, crowned with horns, living in the fires below, like a bourgeois imitation of picturesque old Pluto – that I don't believe. No, I really don't! Heaven and Hell are social concepts created for the sole use of the lower classes and I belong to the middle classes. It's true that I pray to our Lady of Sorrows, for, in just the same way as I pleaded with my teacher to pass me in my final exam and begged the indulgence of a deputy in order to secure my twenty *mil-réis* a month, so I require some super-human protection to keep me safe from consumption and the quinsy, from sharp knives, from the miasmic fevers of the gutter, from the discarded piece of orange peel on which I might slip and break a leg and from various other public ills. Whatever method he uses – be it bowing and scraping or the incensorium – the prudent man paves the way from government ministry to Paradise with a string of judicious blandishments. With a godfather here below and a mystical godmother up above, the fate of the graduate is assured.

And so, unencumbered by any crude superstitions, I felt free to ask that individual all attired in black:

'Do you really think I should ring the bell?'

He raised his hat a little, revealing a narrow brow adorned, like the fabulous Hercules, with a clump of tight black curls, and he replied as follows:

'Let me put it this way, dear Teodoro: a salary of twenty *mil-réis* a month is a social scandal, given the marvels that this world of ours contains. The wines of Burgundy are but one example. Why, an 1858 Romanée-Conti or an 1861 Chambertin would cost, per bottle, between ten and eleven *mil-réis* and, having drunk one glass, there's not a man alive who would hesitate to kill his own father in order to drink another. In Paris and in London they build carriages with such smooth suspension and upholstered in such exquisite fabrics that riding along the Campo Grande in one of them is preferable to travelling through the heavens like the ancient gods on plump cushions of cloud. I won't insult your intelligence by reminding you that today's houses are furnished with such style and comfort as to provide a superior alternative to that fictitious delight, formerly known as "beatitude". Nor will I mention, Teodoro, other earthly delights, for example, the Théâtre Palais Royale, the Ballet Laborde, the Café Anglais . . . I will merely call one fact to your attention: the existence of beings known as Women, quite different from those creatures you have met, who merit only the name of Females. In my day, Teodoro, on page three of the Bible, those beings wore only a fig leaf. Today, Teodoro, their clothes are more like a symphony, a delicate, ingenious poem of laces, batistes, satins, flowers, jewels, cashmeres, gauzes and velvets. Imagine the ineffable pleasure a man could experience just by running the fingers of one hand over such soft marvels; but you must also be aware that you can't pay the bills of such angels with an honest five *tostão* piece. And they possess still more delights, Teodoro. Their hair is either the colour of gold or the colour of night, emblematic of the two great human temptations: the desire for precious metal and the thirst for knowledge of the absolute. And there's more: they have arms the colour of marble, cool as dew-wet lilies; they have breasts on which the great Praxiteles modelled his famous curve, Antiquity's purest and most perfect line, breasts (according to that ingenuous Old Man who shaped them, who made the world, but whose name a centuries-old enmity forbids me to pronounce) which were originally intended for the august nourishment of humanity. But don't worry, Teodoro, nowadays no right-thinking mama would dream of putting them to such harsh and ruinous use; their sole purpose is to be displayed, resplendent, cupped in lace, lit by the gaslight of soirées . . . and for other, more secret uses. Social convention prevents me continuing this joyful enumeration of all the treasures that make up the feminine mystique. Besides, I see there's already a gleam in your eye . . . Now, Teodoro, all these things are beyond the reach, far beyond the reach of your twenty *mil-réis* a month . . . You must at least admit that what I say has the worthy ring of truth about it!'

Face ablaze, I murmured:

'It does.'

And his voice went on, patient and gentle:

'What do you say to a hundred and five or a hundred and six thousand *contos*? A mere bagatelle I know, but at least it's a start, a small aid towards the conquest of happiness. Now, ponder these facts: the Mandarin, that Mandarin in deepest China, is old and gout-ridden. As a man, as a servant of the Celestial Empire, he is about as useful to Peking and to Humanity as a pebble in the mouth of a starving dog. But the transmutation of Matter does exist, of that I can assure you, I who know the innermost secrets of things. For this is how the earth works: it takes the rotting corpse of a man and restores him to the world of living things in the form of a luxuriant plant. It may well be that he, though useless as a mandarin living in the Middle Kingdom, might in another land serve as a perfumed rose or a tasty cabbage. Killing, my son, is almost always a question of balancing universal needs, a question of eliminating excess here in order to supply a lack there. Just ponder this solid philosophy a while. A poor seamstress in London longs to see a flower bloom in the pot of black soil on her garret windowsill. A flower would console that unfortunate woman, but, alas, given the current disposition of beings, the matter that should produce a rose there is still here in the Baixa in the shape of a man of state. But then along comes the thug with his knife at the ready and slices him open. The statesman's guts are washed away with the dirty water in the gutter. He is buried, with carriages in attendance. The matter of which he consists begins to break down, to become part of the vast, evolving world of atoms, and the superfluous statesman, in the form of a pansy, ends up enlivening the blonde seamstress's garret. The assassin is thus a philanthropist! To sum up, Teodoro, the death of that foolish old Mandarin will fill your pockets with a few thousand *contos*. From that moment on, you can thumb your nose at the powers-that-be. Think of the immense pleasure that would give you! You will of course be mentioned in the newspapers: savour that summit of human glory! And think, all you have to do is pick up the bell and ring it. I'm no barbarian; I understand a gentleman's repugnance at the thought of killing a contemporary. The spilling of blood soils the hands with shame and the death throes of a human body are horrible to see. But in this case there will be no such inelegant scenes. It's just like someone summoning a servant. And the result: one hundred and five or one hundred and six thousand *contos*, I can't quite remember how much, but I have it noted down. Trust me, Teodoro. I'm a gentleman, as I proved when, in the war against the tyrant in that first uprising against injustice, I found myself thrown from heights of which even you, sir, cannot conceive. Quite a tumble, I can assure you! Terrible times! What consoles me is that the OTHER was also badly shaken, for when a Jehovah has as his opponent a mere Satan, he can get out of any difficulties simply by calling up another legion of archangels; but when the enemy is a man, armed with a quill pen and an empty notebook, he's lost . . . Anyway, let's call it a hundred and six thousand *contos*. Come on, Teodoro, there's the bell; be a man.'

I know my Christian duty. If that man had led me one moonlit night to the summit of a mountain in Palestine, shown me sleeping cities, peoples and empires, and then said to me sombrely: 'Kill the Mandarin and everything you see on hill and dale will be yours', I would have pointed to the starry heights and, following a famous example, said to him: 'My kingdom is not of this world!' I know my writers. But I was being offered one hundred or so thousand *contos* by the light of a tallow candle, in Travessa da Conceição, by a chap in a tall hat, leaning on an umbrella.

And I did not hesitate. With a steady hand, I rang the bell. Maybe it was an illusion, but it seemed to me that somewhere in the darkness a huge bell, its mouth as vast as the sky itself, tolled across the entire universe in a fearful tone that must surely have woken drowsing suns and portly planets humming on their axes.

The man raised a finger to wipe away the single tear that for a moment dulled his glittering eye:

'Poor Ti Chin-Fu!'

'Is he dead then?'

'He was standing peacefully in his garden, preparing to launch a paper kite into the air, as befits a retired Mandarin, when he was surprised by the ting-a-ling of the bell. Now, on the green grass of the banks of a babbling brook, he lies all dressed in yellow silk, dead, belly uppermost, and in his cold arms he clutches his paper kite, which seems as dead as he is. The funeral will be tomorrow. May the wisdom of Confucius fill him and help his soul on its journey!'

And the man got up, respectfully doffed his hat and left the room with his umbrella under his arm.

When I heard the door slam, I felt as if I were emerging from a nightmare. I ran out into the corridor. A jovial voice was talking to Madame Marques and I heard the wicket gate on the steps click shut. 'Who was that who just went out, Dona Augusta?' I asked, breaking out in a cold sweat.

'It was Cabritinha. He's just popped out for a while to play cards.'

I went back to my room; everything there was calm and real, just as it was normally. The book still lay open at the fearful page. I re-read it. It seemed to me merely the antiquated prose of an old-fashioned moralist, each word dead as an extinguished coal.

I lay down and dreamed that I was far away, somewhere beyond Peking, on the borders of Tartary, in a pavilion in a lamasery, listening to the gentle, prudent maxims, wrapped in the subtle aroma of tea, that flowed from the lips of a living Buddha.

2

A month went by.

I, meanwhile, plodded sadly on in my routine, still placing my italic script at the service of the powers-that-be and, on Sundays, admiring the touching skill with which Dona Augusta massaged away Lieutenant Couceiro's dandruff. I realized what had happened that night: I must have fallen asleep over the book and dreamed my own private version of the Temptation on the Mount. Nevertheless, I instinctively began to take an interest in China. I would go to the Casa Havanesa to read the latest agency bulletins, always on the look-out for news from the Middle Kingdom. It appeared, however, that absolutely nothing was happening in the land of the yellow races. The Havas News Agency merely prattled on about Herzegovina, Bosnia, Bulgaria and other such barbarous oddities.

Little by little, I began to forget the whole fantastic episode but, at the same time, as my spirit gradually regained its composure, the ambitions that had inhabited it before began to stir again: a director-general's salary, Lola's sweet breasts, juicier steaks than those provided by Dona Augusta. But such dreams seemed to me as inaccessible and as insubstantial as the Mandarin's millions. And so, through the monotonous desert of life, the slow caravan of my melancholy thoughts trudged on.

Then one Sunday morning in August, as I was lying stretched out on the bed in my shirtsleeves, dozing, a burned-out cigar in my mouth, I heard the door creak tentatively. Half-opening my drowsy eyes, I saw a bald head at my side, bent in a respectful bow. And then an embarrassed voice murmured:

'Senhor Teodoro? *The* Senhor Teodoro from the Ministry for Internal Affairs and Education?'

I raised myself slowly up on one elbow and answered with a yawn:

'That's me, sir.'

The man's back curved low again, the way a courtier would bow in the august presence of the Clown King Bobèche. The man was extremely short and fat. The ends of his white side whiskers brushed the lapels of his alpaca jacket; a pair of ancient gold-rimmed spectacles gleamed upon his chubby cheeks. He seemed the prosperous personification of Order and yet he was trembling all over, from his shining pate to his calfskin boots. He cleared his throat and stammered:

'I have news for you, sir, great news! My name is Silvestre, of Silvestre, Juliano & Co, your Excellency's humble servant ... The papers just arrived on the steamship from Southampton ... We're representatives for Brito, Alves & Co. of Macau ... agents for Craig & Co. of Hong Kong ... The bills of exchange themselves come from Hong Kong ...'

The man was spluttering now and brandishing in one fat, tremulous hand a plump envelope bearing a black wax seal.

'No doubt,' he went on, 'your Excellency was forewarned of this ... We, however, were not. Our confusion, therefore, is only natural. We hope, however, that your Excellency will continue to look kindly on us. We've always held you in the highest esteem ... You are, in this land of ours, a flower of virtue, a mirror for the righteous! These are the first bank drafts drawn on Baring Brothers of London ... Thirty-day bills of exchange drawn on Rothschild's ...'

At the mention of that name, sonorous as gold itself, I leapt avidly from the bed:

'What *is* all this about, sir?' I shouted.

And he, shouting even louder and waving the envelope, all the time poised on the very tips of his boots, said:

'One hundred and six thousand *contos*, sir! One hundred and six thousand *contos* drawn on the banks of London, Paris, Hamburg and Amsterdam, all in your favour, admirable sir! Yes, in your favour, sir! From the banks of Hong Kong, Shanghai and Canton, from the inheritance deposited there by the Mandarin Ti Chin-Fu!'

I felt the earth tremble beneath my feet and for a second I closed my eyes. But, in a flash, I understood that from that moment on I would be like an incarnation of the Supernatural, drawing from it all my strength and possessed of all its attributes. I could not behave now like a mere man or debase myself by showing human feelings. In order not to disgrace the hieratic line, I even ignored what my own soul cried out to do, which was to go and sob my heart out upon the vast bosom of Madame Marques.

From now on I must show the impassivity of a god – or of a devil. I gave a nonchalant tug at my trousers and addressed these words to Silvestre, Juliano & Co:

'Ah, of course, the Mandarin . . . the Mandarin you mention has behaved like a perfect gentleman. I know what this is all about now, it's a family matter. Leave the papers there, will you . . . Good day.'

Silvestre, Juliano & Co. backed out of the room, his spine bent, his forehead inclined towards the floor.

I went over to the window and opened it wide. Throwing back my head, I breathed in the warm air, relieved, like a weary hind.

Then I looked down at the street where a throng of middle-class folk were trickling quietly out of mass between two lines of carriages. Here and there, quite unconsciously, I found myself noticing women's hairpieces, the gleaming metal on harnesses. And I was suddenly seized by an idea, by a triumphant certainty: that I could hire every one of those carriages by the hour or even by the year if I chose to; that not one of those women would decline to offer up to me her naked breasts were I but to hint at such a desire; that all those men in their Sunday coats would prostrate themselves as if before a Christ, a Mohammed or a Buddha were I to flourish before their eyes the one hundred and six thousand *contos* drawn on all the major banks of Europe!

I leaned on the balustrade and let out a hollow laugh at the sight of the ephemeral bustle of all that servile humanity believing itself to be free and strong, when above, on a fourth-floor balcony, I held in my hand, in an envelope bearing a black seal, the key to their weakness and their slavery! In one voracious leap of the imagination I experienced everything: the pleasures of Luxury, the delights of Love, the arrogance of Power. But the prospect of having the world at my feet provoked in my soul only a great wave of satiety and I yawned like a gorged lion.

What use were those millions if, in the end, all they brought me, day after day, was the painful confirmation of the vileness of the human condition, if, with the shock of all that gold, the moral beauty of the universe vanished before my eyes. I felt gripped by a mystical melancholy. I dropped into a chair, buried my face in my hands and wept bitterly.

Shortly afterwards, Madame Marques, wearing her best black silk, opened the door.

'We're waiting for you to come down to supper, Pipsqueak!'

I emerged from my bitterness only to respond sharply:

'I'm not dining tonight!'

'All the more for us then!'

At that moment I heard rockets exploding in the distance. I remembered that it was Sunday, the day for bullfights, and a sudden vision glittered and flickered before me, drawing me deliciously on: a bullfight viewed from a box seat, then a champagne supper, followed (as an initiation ceremony) by a night of orgies! I ran to the table and stuffed my pockets with London bills of exchange. I raced furiously down the road like a vulture scything through the air towards its prey. An empty calèche went past. I stopped it and cried:

'To the bullfight!'

'That'll be ten *tostões*, sir!'

I looked with repugnance at that despicable piece of organized matter who dared to speak of mere silver coins to a colossus of gold! I plunged my hand into the pocket crammed with all my millions and pulled out the only coins I had: 720 *réis*!

The coachman slapped the horse's rear and drove on, muttering. I stammered out:

'But I've got bills of exchange! Here they are! On London, Hamburg!'

'Come off it!'

Seven hundred and twenty *réis*! And the bulls, the lordly supper, the naked Andalusian women, that whole dream burst like a bubble on the point of a nail.

I hated humanity, I detested money. Another carriage came trotting past, packed with happy people, almost running me over in my distracted state, my seven hundred and twenty *réis* still clutched in my sweaty palm.

Crestfallen, my pockets stuffed with millions courtesy of Rothschild's, I returned to my fourth-floor room. I humbled myself before Madame Marques and accepted the leathery bit of steak she placed before me. I spent that first night of wealth yawning on my solitary bed whilst outside I could hear Couceiro, that happy and insignificant lieutenant with his fifteen *mil-réis* a month, laughing with Dona Augusta and picking out the tune of a *fado* on his guitar.

It was only the following morning while I was shaving that I reflected on the origin of my wealth. It was clearly supernatural and therefore suspect. But, since my rationalism prevented me from attributing those unexpected treasures to the capricious generosity of God or of the Devil, both purely academic fictions, and since the fragments of positivism that form the basis of my philosophy did not encourage any investigation into first causes or essential origins, I quickly decided simply to accept the phenomenon and make good use of it. I therefore ran directly to the London and Brazilian Bank, my jacket flapping in the wind.

Once there, I slapped down on the counter a draft drawn on the Bank of England for a thousand pounds and uttered this one delectable word:

'Gold!'

The cashier suggested gently:

'It might be more convenient in notes.'

'I repeated brusquely:

'Gold!'

I carefully filled my pockets with fistfuls of the stuff and then, laden down, I went out into the street again and hoisted myself into a calèche. I felt fat, obese; I had the taste of gold in my mouth, the dry feel of gold dust on the skin of my hands; the walls of the houses seemed to glitter like tall sheets of gold; and inside my head was the continuous dull murmur of jingling metal, like the motion of a sea in whose waves tumbled ingots of gold.

Abandoning myself to the lurching carriage springs, on which I bounced about as if perched on a rather flabby wineskin, I viewed the street and all the people in it with the bored and bleary eye of one who is tired of life. Then I pushed my hat back on my head, stretched out my legs, stuck out my belly and let out a huge belch, the flatulence of the filthy rich.

I drove around the city like that for a long time, sunk in the stupor of a pleasure-sated nabob. Then a sudden appetite for spending, for squandering gold swelled inside my chest like a gust of wind filling a sail.

'Stop, cur!' I yelled at the coachman.

The pair of horses was reined in. I looked about me with narrowed eyes for something expensive to buy: a precious jewel worthy of a queen perhaps, or a statesman's conscience. I saw nothing and so rushed instead into a tobacconist's.

'Cigars! The more expensive the better!'

'How many, sir?' asked the man in servile tones.

'All of them!' I replied roughly.

At the door, a wretched woman dressed in black with a child asleep at her breast reached out a transparent hand to me. I found it inconvenient having to search for the copper coins amongst all my fistfuls of gold. I pushed her impatiently aside and, pulling my hat down over my eyes, swept coldly out to face the rabble.

It was then that I spotted the ponderous figure of my director-general advancing towards me. At once I found myself with my back bent and my hat, raised in greeting, sweeping the paving stones. It was simply the habit of dependence; all my millions had not yet endowed me with a vertical spine.

Back home I emptied the gold onto my bed and, for a long time, rolled about on top of it, groaning in secret pleasure. The clocktower nearby struck three o'clock and the sun was sinking fast, taking with it my first day of opulence. So, armoured with money, I rushed out to gorge myself!

What a day! I dined in selfish solitude in a private room at the Hotel Central with the table scattered with bottles of wine from Bordeaux, Burgundy, Champagne-Ardennes and the Rhine, as well as liqueurs from every conceivable religious community, as if I were trying to quench a thirty-year-old thirst. In fact the only one I drank to the point of satiety was a local wine from Colares. Then I staggered off to the bordello! What a night! Behind the shutters, the day dawned and I came to stretched out on the carpet, exhausted and half-naked, feeling as if body and soul were evaporating, dissolving, in that sultry atmosphere permeated by the smell of rice powder, women and punch.

When I got back to Travessa da Conceição, the windows of my room were shut and the candle was burning out, flickering palely in its brass holder. Then, when I went over to the bed, this is what I saw: sprawled across the bedspread lay the pot-bellied figure of the Mandarin I had so cruelly cut down. He wore a long pigtail and was dressed in yellow silk and in his arms, as if it too were dead, he held a paper kite!

Desperately, I flung wide the window. The vision disappeared and all that lay on the bed was an old, pale grey overcoat.

3

Then my life as a millionaire really began. I left Madame Marques' house as soon as I could. When she found out I was rich, she spoiled me by giving me rice pudding every day, serving me herself, dressed in her best Sunday silk. I bought and moved into the small yellow palace on Largo do Loreto. The magnificence of my living quarters will be familiar to most readers from the indiscreet engravings published in the magazine *Illustration française*. My bed became famous throughout Europe for its wildly exuberant design, with its carved bedstead covered in gold leaf and its curtains made from rare black brocade on the folds of which I had had erotic verses from Catullus embroidered in pearls. A special lamp lit the interior of the bed with the lovely, milky brilliance of summer moonlight.

I won't deny it, my first months as a rich man were spent in love, my heart beating with all the amorous sincerity of an inexperienced pageboy. The first time I set eyes on her was like a vignette in a novel: she was watering the carnations on her balcony. Her name was Cândida, she was very small and blonde and she lived on Rua de Buenos Aires in a chaste little house all overgrown with creepers. Her graceful, slender waist reminded me of all Art's finest, most fragile creations – Mimi, Virginie, Joaninha from the Vale de Santarém.

Each night I would fall in mystical ecstasy at her feet, which were pale as marble, and each morning I would fill her lap with 20-*mil réis* notes, which she would refuse at first with a blush, then put away in a drawer, calling me Totó, her angel.

One day, I tiptoed into her boudoir unannounced, across the thick Syrian carpet. She was sitting there writing, deep in thought, one little finger in the air. When she saw me, she went pale and trembled, and tried to hide the paper that bore her monogram. I snatched it from her in a fit of foolish jealousy. It was the usual letter, the inevitable letter, the letter that women have written ever since Antiquity: it began 'My idol' and was addressed to a second lieutenant who lived around the corner.

I plucked love from my breast as if it were a poisonous plant. I lost for ever my faith in blonde angels, who preserve in their blue eyes a trace of the heavens they have gazed upon. Perched on my pile of gold, I unleashed the bitter laughter of Mephistopheles upon Innocence, Modesty and all other such unfortunate ideals and coldly created for myself a purely carnal existence, grandiose and cynical.

On the stroke of midday, I would step into my pink marble bath sprinkled with perfumes that lent the water the opacity of milk. Young pages, with soft hands, would rub me down with a ceremonious respect usually reserved for acts of worship. Then, wrapped in a dressing gown of Indian silk, flanked on either side by silent lackeys, I would walk along the gallery, glancing now and then at the paintings by Fortuny and by Corot, heading for my steak *à l'anglaise*, served up on blue and gold Sèvres.

If the day was hot, I would spend it reclining on cushions made of satin the colour of pearls, in a boudoir furnished with fine Dresden china and enough flowers to make a garden worthy of Tasso's Armida. There I would linger over the *Diário de Notícias*, whilst lovely girls dressed in Japanese costumes cooled the air with feathered fans.

In the evening I would go for a walk as far as Pote das Almas. That was the most tedious part of the day. I would stroll along leaning on my walking stick, dragging my indolent feet, giving great yawns like a beast replete from the kill, and the abject masses would stop and stare in astonishment at the sight of this bored nabob!

Sometimes I felt almost nostalgic for the days when I was busy at the office. I would go home and shut myself up in the library, where the Great Thoughts of Mankind waited, forgotten and bound in Morocco leather, and I would sharpen a quill and spend hours writing out on the same beloved paper I had used at work: *Esteemed Sir, I have the honour to inform you . . ., I have the pleasure of sending Your Honour . . ., Illustrious Sir . . .*

As night fell, a servant would announce supper by playing a Gothic melody on a silver tuba, which would echo down all the corridors. I would rise and dine in majestic solitude. Silent as gliding shadows, a horde of lackeys in black silk livery would serve me with rare victuals and wines the price of jewels. The whole table would be resplendent with flowers, lights, crystals and gleaming gold but, subtle as mist, curling about the pyramids of fruit and mingling with the steam from the plates, hung an errant air of unspeakable tedium.

Afterwards I would heave my bloated body into my carriage seat and set off for Rua das Janelas Verdes, where I kept a bevy of women in the most exquisite Islamic style, in a garden fit for a sultan's seraglio. They would dress me in a tunic of cool, perfumed silk, and I would abandon myself to the basest of passions. At the first light of dawn, I would be borne home, half-dead. Mechanically I would make my usual sign of the cross but would soon be flat on my back snoring, deathly pale and bathed in a cold sweat, like an exhausted Tiberius.

Meanwhile Lisbon threw itself at my feet. The courtyard of the palace was constantly packed with mobs of people. I watched, bored, from the windows of the gallery. I saw the gleaming shirtfronts of the Aristocracy, the black soutanes of the Clergy and the shining, sweaty faces of the Plebs. With abject words on their lips, they all came to beg me to honour them with a smile and a share in my gold. Sometimes I would agree to receive some old man with a historic title. He would advance across the floor, his white hair almost brushing the ground, stammering out adulatory phrases. As he pressed to his heart a hand through whose thick veins ran the blood of three centuries, he had no hesitation in offering me a much-loved daughter as a wife or even as a concubine.

Everyone brought gifts as if to an idol on an altar. Some brought me votive verses, some brought slippers or cigarette-holders, others my monogram embroidered in hair, but each

36

brought me his or her conscience. If my dull eye fell by chance on a woman in the street, the very next day there would be a letter from the creature, regardless of whether she was someone's wife or a prostitute, offering me her nakedness, her love and all the pleasures of the flesh.

Journalists plundered their imaginations to find adjectives worthy of my greatness. I was 'the sublime Senhor Teodoro', even 'the celestial Senhor Teodoro', then, in a moment of madness, the *Gazeta das Locais*, called me 'the extracelestial Senhor Teodoro'! Not one head remained covered in my presence, regardless of whether that head wore a crown or a bowler hat. Each day I was offered the presidency of some ministry or the directorship of a guild. I always refused in disgust.

Gradually, the news of my wealth spread beyond the borders of the kingdom. The courtly *Figaro* spoke of me in every issue, preferring me to the pretender, Henri V. The immortal grotesque who signs himself 'Saint-Genest' wrote exhortatory articles begging me to save France and it was then that the foreign illustrated magazines first published, in full colour, scenes from my life. I received envelopes bearing heraldic seals from all the princesses of Europe, revealing to me, in photographs and documents, both their physical attractions and the antiquity of their family trees. Two quips I happened to make that year were telegraphed to the universe via the wires of the Havas News Agency and were considered wittier than anything said by Voltaire or Rochefort or by that fine wit known as 'Everyman'. I only had to break wind for the whole of humanity to read about it in the newspapers. I lent money to kings, I subsidised civil wars and I was swindled by all the South American republics around the Gulf of Mexico.

And yet I was sad . . .

Every time I went into my house I was brought up short, trembling, by the same vision: stretched across the threshold or across my golden bed, there lay the pot-bellied figure, with his black pigtail and yellow tunic, his kite in his arms. The

37

Mandarin Ti Chin-Fu! I would rush towards him, my fist raised and he would vanish.

Then I would fall into an armchair, prostrated and bathed in sweat, and in the silent room, where the light from the candles in the chandeliers danced blood red on the scarlet damasks, I would murmur:

'I must kill that corpse!'

However, it was not the impudence of that plump ghost, making himself at home amongst my furniture, on my bedspreads, that was souring my life.

The supreme horror consisted in the idea that fixed itself in my mind like a blade that could not be shifted: *I had murdered an old man!*

I had not done so by putting a rope around his neck, Muslim-style, nor, in the Italian style of the Renaissance, by poisoning a chalice of Syracuse wine nor by using one of the classical methods, tried and tested throughout the history of kings – Dom João II's dagger, Charles IX's rifle . . .

I had got rid of the creature, from afar, with a bell. It was absurd, fantastic, even amusing. But it did not detract from the tragic blackness of the fact: *I had murdered an old man!*

This certainty gradually grew and hardened in my soul like a stone. It dominated my whole inner life like a pillar set in an open plain, so much so that, however roundabout a route I took, my thoughts always returned to that accusing memory blackening the horizon. However high my imagination flew, it always ended up bruising its wings on that monument to moral poverty.

Ah, however much one may consider Life and Death to be but banal transmutations of Matter, it is still terrifying to think that one has made warm blood freeze and living muscle grow still! After supper, with the smell of good coffee beside me, I had only to stretch out on a sofa, languid and replete, for a murmur of accusing voices to rise up inside me, as melancholy as the chorus of cries from a prison:

'And yet it was you who ensured that this same well-being in which you now revel would never more be enjoyed by the venerable Ti Chin-Fu!'

In vain I tried to answer back, reminding my Conscience of the Mandarin's decrepitude, of his incurable gout. Eloquent in argument, greedy for discussion, it would reply with fury:

'However limited its activity, life is still the supreme good, for its charm lies in its very existence and not in the multiplicity of its outward manifestations!'

I rebelled against the rhetorical pedantry of that rigid pedagogue. My head high, I yelled back at my Conscience in tones of desperate arrogance:

'All right, I did kill him! Is that better? What more do you want? I'm not frightened of the great name you bear! You're just a figment of my own nervous sensibility. All I need to get rid of you is a little orangeflower water!'

And at once, passing through my soul with the slowness of a breeze, I would hear a humble murmur of ironic comments:

'Fine, then, eat, sleep, bathe, make love . . .'

And so I did. But soon, before my horrified gaze, even the Breton linen sheets on my bed took on the pallid tones of a winding sheet. The perfumed water into which I plunged myself cooled thickly on my skin like coagulating blood and the bare breasts of my lovers saddened me as if they were the marble slabs covering a corpse.

Then a greater sadness assaulted me. It occurred to me that Ti Chin-Fu would have had a vast family with grandchildren and little great-grandchildren. In China, deprived of the inheritance that I was busy devouring off my Sèvres dishes with all the pomp of a wastrel sultan, they would be suffering all the usual torments of human poverty – days without rice, their bodies unclothed, their pleas for alms rejected, with only the muddy road to call their home . . .

I understood then why the plump figure of the old scholar kept pursuing me and I thought I heard this bleak accusation issue from those lips hidden by the white hair of his ghostly beard: 'It's not for myself that I mourn, I was as good as dead anyway. No, I weep for the poor unfortunates you ruined and who, at this very moment, whilst you come fresh from the cool breasts of your lovers, are whimpering with hunger, shivering with cold, huddled together to die amongst lepers and thieves on the Bridge of Beggars, near the terraces of the Temple of Heaven!'

An ingenious torture, worthy of the Chinese! I could not raise a piece of bread to my lips without at once imagining the sufferings of that starving band of little children, the descendants of Ti Chin-Fu, like featherless nestlings in an abandoned nest, vainly opening their beaks and calling out. If I felt too hot in my overcoat, I would immediately be filled by visions of unfortunate ladies on snowy mornings, accustomed to warm Chinese comforts but now blue with cold, clothed only in the ragged remains of old silk dresses. The ebony ceiling of my palace made me think of the Mandarin's family sleeping beside canals, nosed and sniffed at by dogs, and my well-upholstered coupé made me shiver at the thought of those long, aimless treks along waterlogged roads, in a harsh Asian winter.

How I suffered! And yet, outside, the envious rabble would gather to gaze in wonder at my palace, speculating on the inaccessible joys it must contain!

At last, recognizing that my Conscience was lodged inside me like an angry snake, I decided to ask for help from that Being said to be superior to Conscience because possessed of the gift of Grace.

Unfortunately, I did not believe in Him. So I resorted instead to my own private divinity, to my favourite idol, my family's personal patroness: Our Lady of Sorrows. And in city cathedrals and village chapels a whole tribe of priests and canons (all magnificently rewarded for their efforts) busied themselves in praying to Our Lady of Sorrows that she might turn her pitying gaze on my inner ills. But no relief came from those inclement Heavens to which, for thousands of years, the warmth of human misery has risen in vain.

Then I myself plunged into pious practices and Lisbon was witness to the most extraordinary spectacle: a wealthy man, a nabob, prostrating himself humbly at the foot of altars, holding up his hands in prayer and stammering out words from the Hail Mary, as if he saw in Prayer and the Kingdom of Heaven, which can be conquered by Prayer, something more than a fictitious consolation invented by those who have everything in order to keep those who have nothing contented. I belong to the bourgeoisie and I know that the only reason my class bothers to show the lower classes that distant Paradise full of ineffable pleasures that will one day be theirs is to divert attention from our own bulging coffers and from the abundance of our harvests.

Still feeling uneasy and still hoping to placate the wandering soul of Ti Chin-Fu, I ordered thousands of masses, plain and sung. The childish folly of a peninsular mind! For the old Mandarin, in his role as scholar, member of the Han-Lin Academy, probable collaborator on the great 'Khu Tsuane-Chu' treatise, which already comprises some seventy-eight thousand seven hundred and thirty volumes, would almost certainly have been a follower of the Confucianist doctrine of active morality. He would never even have burned perfumed joss sticks in honour of the Buddha and, to his abominable, sceptical grammarian's soul, rituals of mystical sacrifice must have seemed akin to the dumb show put on by the clowns in the Hong-Tung theatre!

Then, various astute prelates of wide experience gave me some clever advice: I should try to gain the good will of Our Lady of Sorrows with presents, flowers, brocades and jewels, as if I were trying to win the favours of Aspasia. So I attempted to bribe the sweet Mother of all Men, like some fat banker trying to win over a dancer by buying her a cottage in the country, and in response to that priestly suggestion, I had a cathedral built, made entirely of white marble. The sheer abundance of flowers placed amongst the carved pillars was reminiscent of scenes from Paradise, and the multiplicity of candles recalled the magnificence of the stars. All in vain! The fine, erudite Cardinal Nani came all the way from Rome to consecrate the church, but when I went that day to visit my divine hostess, I saw above the bald heads of the celebrants, amidst the mystic clouds of incense, not the fair Queen of Grace in her blue tunic but that old rascal with his slanting eyes and his kite clutched in his arms! A whole priesthood dripping in gold, accompanied by the growl of the organ, was

41

offering up an Eternity of praise to *him*, to his drooping white moustaches and his ochre yellow belly.

Thinking that perhaps it was Lisbon and the stagnant milieu in which I moved that was helping to generate such imaginings, I left, travelling discreetly, without pomp, with just one trunk and a servant.

I visited, in the traditional order, first Paris, then banal Switzerland, followed by London and the taciturn lochs of Scotland. I pitched my tent outside the evangelical walls of Jerusalem and travelled the length of that sad, monumental land of Egypt, like a corridor in a mausoleum, from Alexandria to Thebes. Despite being seasick on steamships and enduring the monotony of ruins, the melancholy of unknown multitudes and the disappointments of the boulevard, my inner malaise continued to grow.

It was no longer just the bitter knowledge that I had disinherited a respectable family that filled me with remorse. I felt doubly guilty for having deprived a whole society of an important personage, an experienced man of letters, a pillar of the Social Order, a mainstay of public institutions. You can't just remove a man worth one hundred and six thousand *contos* from a country without upsetting the balance. I was tormented by this idea. I longed to know if the disappearance of Ti Chin-Fu really had proved disastrous for old China. I read all the newspapers from Hong Kong and Shanghai; I spent whole nights poring over travel books; I consulted wise missionaries; and every article, man and book spoke to me of the decadence of the Middle Kingdom, of ruined provinces, dying cities, starving peasants, plagues, rebellions, crumbling temples, the undermining of the authority of the law, the disintegration of a whole world, like a ship run aground and being undone plank by plank by the waves.

And I attributed the misfortunes of Chinese society to myself. In my sick mind Ti Chin-Fu had taken on the disproportionate worth of a Caesar, a Moses, one of those providential beings who are the very strength of a race. I had killed him and with him had disappeared the vitality of a whole nation! At one brilliant stroke, his vast brain might perhaps have saved that old Asiatic monarchy and I had checked that creative impulse! His fortune would have contributed to shoring up the wealth of the Exchequer and here I was squandering it by giving peaches in January to the Messalinas of the Café Helder. My friends, I felt the terrible remorse of one responsible for having ruined a whole empire!

In order to try and forget this complicated torment I gave myself up to orgies. I moved into a large house on the Champs-Elysées and what followed was truly horrendous. I would hold parties that outdid Trimalchio in their extravagance and, at the height of this libertine frenzy, when brass bands would be blasting out the brutal cadences of the cancan, when bare-breasted prostitutes would be shrieking out the filthiest of songs and my Bohemian guests, beerhall atheists to a man, would be raising their champagne glasses and raining down curses on God, then I, seized like Heliogabalus by a fury of bestiality, by a hatred for all thought and consciousness, would hurl myself to the floor on all fours and bray loudly like a donkey.

But I wanted to sink still further, to the debauchery of the lower classes, to the alcoholic depravities of the grogshop, so I would dress up in a smock, a cap pushed back on my head, and go off with my drunken horde, staggering arm in arm along the outlying boulevards with Mes-Bottes or Bibi-la-Gaillarde, belching and bawling out:

> *Allons, enfants de la patrie-e-e!*
> *Le jour de gloire est arrivé . . .*

Then one morning, after one of those nights of excess, at that hour when a vague spiritual dawn sometimes fills the darkness of the soul of the debauchee, the idea of going to China was born. And, like soldiers sleeping in their camp, who arise at the sound of the clarion and form up one by one into a marching column, so other ideas gathered in my spirit, lining up to make a formidable plan. I would leave for Peking; I would search out the family of Ti Chin-Fu, marry one of the ladies of the house, thus legitimizing my possession of his millions; I would return that learned house to its old prosperity; I would hold grand funeral ceremonies for the Mandarin in order to calm his restless spirit; I would travel through the poverty-stricken provinces distributing massive quantities of rice, and, having secured the title of Mandarin from the emperor himself, an easy task for a graduate like myself, I would replace the vanished Ti Chin-Fu and thus restore to his country, if not the authority of his wisdom, at least the might of his gold.

Sometimes, this all struck me as an entirely ill-conceived plan, vague, puerile and idealistic. But I was gripped by the desire to set off on that original and epic adventure and I allowed myself to be carried along by it, like a dry leaf by a gust of wind.

All I longed and sighed for was to set foot in China! One night, after complex preparations, helped along by handfuls of gold, I finally left en route for Marseilles. I had hired a whole steamship, the *Ceylon*, and the following morning, on an electric blue sea, beneath the circling white wings of seagulls, when the first pink rays of the sun touched the towers of Notre-Dame-de-la-Garde perched on its dark rock, I set our prow for the Orient.

4

The voyage to Shanghai on the *Ceylon* proved calm and monotonous and we journeyed from there up the Blue River to Tientsin in a small steamer belonging to the Russell Company. I had not come to visit China as a tourist, out of idle curiosity, and I felt glumly indifferent to the landscape of that province, which resembled the misty blue landscapes painted on porcelain vases, full of low hills, bare but for the waving branches of an occasional tree.

As we passed Nanking, the captain of the steamer, an impudent Yankee with a face like a goat, suggested that we stop to visit the monumental ruins of the old city of porcelain, but I refused with a terse shake of my head, not even raising my sad eyes from the muddy waters of the river.

The days spent travelling from Tientsin to Tung-Chu in flat-bottomed boats rowed by stinking Chinamen were dreary and tedious. We passed low-lying areas flooded by the Pei-Hó as well as endless, pale paddy fields. Here and there we saw a gloomy village built out of black mud or a field strewn with yellow coffins and we constantly came across the swollen, green corpses of beggars drifting slowly downstream beneath lowering skies.

In Tung-Chu I was surprised to be met by an escort of Cossacks sent to greet me by old General Camilloff, a hero of the campaigns in Central Asia and, at the time, Russian ambassador to Peking. I had been commended to his care as if I were some rare and precious creature. The garrulous interpreter Sá-Tó, whom he had placed at my service, explained to me that the letters bearing the imperial seal advising Camilloff of my arrival had been received some weeks before through the Chancery postal system, by which letters cross Siberia by sleigh, are then transported by camel as far as the Great Wall and handed over to Mongolian horsemen dressed in scarlet leather, who ride day and night until they reach Peking.

Camilloff had sent me a Manchurian pony caparisoned in silk and a visiting card with these words written in pencil beneath his name: Greetings! The pony has a soft mouth!

I mounted the pony and, with a hurrah from the Cossacks and much heroic brandishing of lances, we set off at a gallop across the dusty plain, for evening was already falling and the gates of Peking are shut the moment the last ray of sun leaves the towers of the Temple of Heaven. At first, we followed a path, a track beaten hard by the constant traffic of caravans and strewn with vast, loose slabs of marble from what had once been the Imperial Way. Then we crossed the bridge of Pa Li-Kao, built all of white marble and flanked by proud dragons. We galloped along canals of black water, past orchards and, now and then, came across a village, almost blue in colour, nestling at the foot of a pagoda. Then, at a bend in the road, I stopped, astonished.

Peking lay before me! Its vast wall, monumental and pitiless, dull black in colour, disappeared off into the distance. The extravagant architecture of its ornate gateways stood silhouetted against a sunset of sanguine reds and purples. Far off towards the north, in a haze of violet mist, hanging as if suspended in mid-air, were the mountains of Mongolia.

At the Gate of Tung Tsen-Men a splendid litter was waiting to carry me across Peking to Camilloff's military residence. Seen from close to, the Wall seemed to rise up to the heavens like some awesome biblical structure. At its foot clustered a jumble of huts, an exotic market filled by the buzz of voices, where swinging lanterns were already staining the twilight with vague smudges of blood-red light and the white awnings at the foot of the black wall looked like a cloud of resting butterflies.

I felt sad as I got into the litter. I drew the curtains of scarlet, gold-embroidered silk and then, surrounded by Cossacks, I entered old Peking through that Babel of a gate, plunging into the tumultuous rabble, past carts, sedan chairs, Mongolian horsemen armed with arrows, monks in pure white tunics marching in single file and long lines of slow dromedaries, their loads swaying rhythmically.

The litter soon came to a halt. Sá-Tó, ever respectful, drew back the curtains, and I found myself in a dark, silent garden where brightly lit pavilions glowed gently beneath the ancient sycamores like huge lanterns placed upon the grass and where a multitude of streams murmured as they flowed through the shadows. Beneath a colonnade of vermilion-painted wood hung with garlands of paper lights, a fine figure of a man stood waiting for me. He had a white moustache and was leaning on a heavy sword. It was General Camilloff. As I approached him, I heard the flurry of gazelles running lightly away through the trees.

The old hero clasped me to his chest for a moment and then, in accordance with Chinese custom, offered me the bath of hospitality, a vast porcelain tub of lilac-scented water bobbing with white sponges and thin slices of lemon.

The moon was already filling the gardens with delicious light when Camilloff led me, refreshed and in white tie and tails, into his wife's private sitting room. His wife was tall and blonde with the green eyes of one of Homer's sirens. A single scarlet rose rested in the décolletage of her white silk dress and the subtle perfume of sandalwood and tea lingered about her fingers, which I kissed.

We talked a lot about Europe, about nihilism, Zola, Leo XIII and how thin Sarah Bernhardt had become.

As a warm breeze wafted the scent of heliotrope along the open gallery, the General's wife sat down at the piano and, until late into the night, her contralto voice broke the melancholy silence of the Tartar City with saucy arias from *Madame Favart* and soothing melodies from *Le Roi de Lahore*.

Closeted with the General early next morning, in one of the pavilions in the garden, I recounted my whole painful story and the bizarre motives that had brought me to Peking. The great hero listened, sombrely stroking his thick Cossack moustache.

'Does my honoured guest know Chinese?' he asked suddenly, fixing me with an astute eye.

'I know two important words, General: "Mandarin" and "chá".'

He passed a thickly veined hand over the hideous scar furrowing his bald head:

' "Mandarin", my friend, is not a Chinese word and no one in China knows what it means. It's the name the sixteenth-century navigators from your country, from your beautiful country . . .'

'. . . in the days when we had navigators,' I murmured, sighing.

Out of politeness, he sighed too and then went on:

'It's the name that your navigators gave to Chinese officials. It comes from the verb, that lovely verb of yours . . .'

'. . . in the days when we had verbs,' I muttered, slipping instinctively into the national habit of running down my homeland.

His eyes, round as an owl's, went momentarily blank and then he continued, patiently and seriously:

'From that lovely verb of yours "mandar" – to command. So that leaves you with the word for tea, "chá", a word that does indeed play an immensely important role in Chinese life, but would still not be enough, I fear, to deal with all social occasions. My honoured guest wishes to marry a lady from Ti Chin-Fu's family, to continue the vast influence exercised by the Mandarin, to replace the late lamented gentleman both domestically and socially, and to achieve this, all you have is the word "chá". It's not very much.'

I could not deny it, it really wasn't very much. Wrinkling his great hooked nose, the worthy Russian set out further objections that rose up between me and my desires like the great wall of Peking itself: no lady from Ti Chin-Fu's family would ever consent to marry a barbarian and it would be impossible, unthinkable, for the emperor, the Child of the Sun, to bestow on a foreigner the honours and privileges of a Mandarin.

'But why would he refuse to give them to me?' I exclaimed. 'I come from a good family in the province of Minho. I'm a graduate and that makes me as much a man of letters in China as it does in Coimbra! I've already worked in a government department. I'm extremely rich. I know about administration . . .'

The General bowed respectfully before the sheer abundance of my attributes.

At last, he said: 'It isn't that the emperor would refuse them to you exactly, it's just that the person who proposed it to him would be immediately beheaded. Chinese law is both explicit and brutal on this point.'

I lowered my head, dispirited.

'But, General,' I murmured, 'I want to free myself from the hateful presence of old Ti Chin-Fu and his kite! Since I cannot become a Mandarin and use my personal wealth to increase the prosperity of the State, what if I gave half of all my millions to the Chinese treasury? Perhaps that would placate Ti Chin-Fu.'

The General placed a vast, fatherly hand on my shoulder.

'That would be a mistake, my boy, a grave mistake! Those millions would never reach the imperial Treasury. They would line the bottomless pockets of the ruling classes. They would be frittered away on planting gardens, collecting porcelain, buying animal skins to cover their floors, clothing concubines in silks. They would not help to relieve the hunger of a single ordinary Chinese person, nor repair one stone along the public highways. They would merely con- tribute to the continuance of the whole Asian orgy. The soul of Ti Chin-Fu must know the Empire well. No, no, that would never satisfy him.'

'And what if I used part of the old devil's fortune to distribute generous amounts of rice to the starving populace, as a private act of philanthropy? That's an idea, isn't it?'

'A terrible one,' said the General, frowning dreadfully. 'The imperial court would immediately perceive that as evidence of political ambition, as a devious plan to gain the favour of the people, a threat to the Dynasty . . . You, my good friend, would be beheaded. Awful . . .'

'Good God!' I shouted. 'Then what did I come to China for?'

The diplomat shrugged nonchalantly and gave a knowing smile that revealed yellow Cossack teeth:

'What you *can* do is find Ti Chin-Fu's family. I'll ascertain from the prime minister, His Excellency Prince Tong, the whereabouts of the particular brood you're interested in. You can then gather them all together, shower a few millions on them, and organize a splendid funeral for the dead man, a funeral of great pomp and ceremony, with a cortège a league long, with columns of monks, a whole army of banners, palanquins, lances, feathers, scarlet biers, legions of professional mourners wailing dolefully, etc. etc. If, after all that, your conscience is still not at peace and the ghost continues to pester you . . .'

'What then?'

'You'd best cut your throat.'

'Thank you, General.'

One thing was clear, however, and on that Camilloff, his wife and the ever-respectful Sá-Tó were all in agreement: if I was to visit Ti Chin-Fu's family, arrange the funeral and integrate myself into life in Peking, I should start dressing like a wealthy Chinaman of the literate classes, in order to accustom myself to the different clothes and manners, to Mandarin etiquette.

My rather sallow complexion and my long, drooping moustaches helped in the disguise and, on the following morning, having been dressed by the ingenious tailors of Chá-Cua Street, I entered the room lined with scarlet silk, where the dishes for lunch were already gleaming on the black lacquer table, and the General's wife stepped back as if Tong-Tché himself, the Son of Heaven, had appeared before her.

I was wearing a tunic of dark blue brocade buttoned at the side. The front was richly embroidered with gold dragons and flowers. Over that, in a paler shade of blue, I wore a short, full coat in very soft silk. My nut-brown satin trousers revealed splendid yellow slippers sewn with pearls and a glimpse of stocking sprinkled with tiny black stars. And, at the waist, tucked into a charming belt fringed with silver, I carried a bamboo fan of the kind they make in Swa-ton, bearing a portrait of the philosopher Lao-Tzu.

In the mysterious way clothes have of influencing one's personality, I could already feel Chinese ideas and instincts stirring within me: a love of meticulous ceremonies, a bureaucratic respect for formulae, a touch of learned scepticism combined with an abject terror of the emperor, a hatred of foreigners, a belief in ancestor worship, a fanatical love of tradition and a taste for sugary foods.

I was already a Mandarin, body and soul. I did not greet the General's wife with: *Bonjour, Madame*, instead, bending from the waist, I pressed my clenched fists to my temples and made a low bow chin-chin style. 'You look adorable, just delightful!' she said, smiling her lovely smile and clapping her small, pale hands.

That day, in honour of my new incarnation, we had a Chinese lunch with charming scarlet napkins made out of tissue paper with fabulous monsters drawn on them in black. The lunch began with oysters from Ning-Pó, which were excellent! I swallowed down two dozen of them with intense, Chinese delight. Then came a delicious sharkfin soup, sheep's eyes in garlic sauce, a dish of waterlilies in sugar syrup, oranges from Canton and, finally, the obligatory rice, the rice of the ancestors. A superb meal, liberally washed down with excellent wine from Chão-Chigne. And finally, the pleasure of receiving my glass of boiling water and placing in it a pinch of imperial tea leaves from the first harvest of March, a unique harvest picked by the pure hands of virgins as part of a holy ritual!

While we smoked, two women singers came in, accompanied by two Tartars, who sat crosslegged, strumming out wild, melancholy rhythms on guitars covered in snakeskin. In guttural tones, the women sang ancient songs that dated back to the Ming Dynasty. China certainly contains some very rare delights.

Afterwards, the General's blonde wife gave a very witty rendition of 'Femme à Barbe' and, when the General had left with his Cossack escort in order to visit Prince Tong's office and discover the whereabouts of the Ti Chin-Fu family, I, feeling replete and in an excellent mood, sallied forth with Sá-Tó to see Peking.

Camilloff's residence was in the Tartar City, in the district reserved for the military and the nobility. An austere calm reigns there. The streets are like the long, rutted paths of a village and tend to hug the contours of walls shaded by the broad branches of sycamore trees.

Sometimes, a carriage rushes past pulled by a Mongol pony at full trot, the high carriage wheels studded with golden nails. Everything in it trembles: the awning, the silk curtains, the bunches of feathers at each corner, and inside you glimpse some lovely Chinese lady, clothed in pale brocades, her hair full of flowers, jingling the two silver bracelets on her wrist with an air of ceremonious tedium. Then along comes a Mandarin's sedan chair carried by coolies dressed all in blue, their pigtails flying, racing along at a gruelling pace to the offices of the State. They are preceded by a tattered band of servants bearing silk scrolls embroidered with inscriptions, the insignia of authority, whilst inside, the potbellied dignitary, wearing huge, round glasses, riffles through his papers or dozes with his mouth open.

We kept stopping to look in at the splendid shops with their vertical signs painted in gold on a scarlet background. Subtle as shadows, in a reverent silence, the customers examine the precious merchandise: Ming dynasty porcelain, enamels, ivory, silks, weapons decorated with inlaid work and marvellous fans from Swa-Ton. A sturdy, young girl with slanting eyes, wearing a blue tunic and paper poppies in her plaits, occasionally unrolls some rare brocade for the benefit of a stout Chinaman, who regards it solemnly, his fingers laced across his belly. In the background, the merchant, with magnificent impassivity, is writing with a brush on long strips of sandalwood, and a sweet perfume, emanating from the things themselves, troubles and saddens the spirit.

And there stands the wall surrounding the Forbidden City, the holy dwelling of the emperor! Noble young men were coming down from the terrace of a temple where they had been practising archery. Sá-Tó told me their names; they belonged to the special ceremonial guard in charge of escorting the yellow silk sunshade embroidered with the dragon that is the sacred emblem of the emperor. They all bowed low to an old man with a venerable beard, wearing the short yellow jacket which is the privilege of the old. He was strolling along talking to himself and carried a stick on which tame skylarks perched. He was a prince of the Empire.

Such strange places! But I enjoyed nothing so much as the recurring sight of two paunchy Mandarins meeting at a garden gate, who, before they could enter, had to go through a whole rigid ceremony involving the exchange of endless salaams, bows, retreats and peals of polite high-pitched laughter that set the long peacock feathers on their backs trembling in the most comical fashion. Then, if you looked up, you would see huge paper kites hovering in the air, some in the shape of dragons or whales, others in the shape of fabulous birds, filling the sky with a fantastic swarm of swaying, transparent monsters.

'Sá-Tó, that's enough of the Tartar City! Let's go and see the Chinese area.'

And off we went through the monstrous Tchin-Men gate into the Chinese City, where the bourgeoisie, the tradesmen and the ordinary people live. Its streets are arranged like lines on a page and here and there along the ancient, muddy byways, formed over the centuries out of the compacted detritus of generations, you could still sometimes see a slab of the pink marble that paved the streets in former times, during the great Ming dynasty.

On either side of the streets there were empty plots of land filled by howling bands of starving dogs, rows of melancholy shacks or squalid shops with their thin, rust-flecked signs swaying on iron poles. In the distance we saw triumphal arches made from purple-painted beams topped by an oblong roof of varnished blue tiles that gleamed like enamel. A dense, noisy crowd, dressed mainly in brown and blue tunics, milled ceaselessly about. The dust wrapped everything in a yellow mist, an acrid stench rose from the black streams of water and endless caravans of camels led by sombre Mongols, clad in sheepskins, pushed their way slowly through the mob.

We went as far as the bridges over the canals, where half-naked mountebanks, wearing masks representing terrifying demons, perform tricks outlandish in their subtlety. And I stood for a long time admiring the astrologers in their long tunics with paper dragons fastened to their backs, loudly touting horoscopes and consultations with the stars. It truly is a fabulous and unique city!

Then there was a sudden clamour of voices! We ran to see what it was and saw a band of prisoners, tied to each other by their pigtails, whom a soldier wearing large spectacles was driving along with prods from his sunshade! It was there, on that same avenue, that I witnessed the noisy funeral procession of a Mandarin, all hung about with oriflammes and streamers. Groups of mournful people were walking along carrying smoking tapers in portable burners. Women in rags rolled about on carpets, howling with grief, then got up and stood joking amongst themselves whilst a coolie, dressed in white mourning, served them tea from a huge pot shaped like a bird.

When we passed the Temple of Heaven, I saw an army of beggars crowded into a square, their only covering a tile tied around their waist by a piece of string. The women, with faded paper flowers woven into their hair, were calmly gnawing on bones while the corpses of children rotted nearby beneath the buzz of blowflies. Further on, we came across a cage containing a condemned man who stuck his scrawny hands through the bars to beg for alms. Then Sá-Tó showed me a narrow square where small cages had been placed on the tops of stone pillars. They contained decapitated heads from which thick, black blood dripped down, drop by slow drop.

'Ooph!' I exclaimed, weary and overwhelmed. 'What I'd like now, Sá-Tó, is rest, silence and an expensive cigar.'

He bowed and led me up a granite staircase to the high walls of the city that formed an esplanade broad enough for four chariots of war to run alongside each other for several leagues.

And whilst Sá-Tó sat down in a gap in the battlements, yawning the yawn of the bored guide, I smoked my cigar and contemplated the vast city of Peking that lay at my feet.

It was like one of those terrifying cities in the Bible, Babel or Nineveh, which the prophet Jonah took three days to cross. The horizon, transparent in the distant blue air, was dominated in every direction by the great square wall, with its gates and their massive towers. Within the immense area it enclosed lay a confused jumble of green woods, artificial lakes, steel-bright canals, marble bridges, fields strewn with ruins and varnished rooftops shining in the sunlight. Everywhere there were heraldic pagodas, the white terraces of temples, triumphal arches and innumerable pavilions set in leafy gardens. Then there were areas that looked like nothing so much as piles of porcelain, others that resembled heaps of mud . . . but one's eye always came back, again and again, to the mighty battlements in all their splendour.

Beside these grandiose structures, the crowds looked like grains of black sand blown hither and thither by a gentle breeze.

The vast imperial palace with its roof the yellow of bright gold lay among mysterious groves of trees! How I longed to penetrate its secrets and see, unfolding along the many-tiered galleries, the barbarous splendour of those centuries-old dynasties.

Beyond rose the tower of the Temple of Heaven, like three sunshades placed one on top of the other, then the great Column of the Principles, grave and hieratical as the spirit of the race itself, and beyond that, the pale, eerie half-tints of the jasper terraces of the Sanctuary of Purification.

Then, in answer to my questions, Sá-Tó and his respectful finger pointed out to me the Temple of the Imperial Ancestors, the Palace of Supreme Harmony, the Pavilion of the Flowers of Literature and the Pavilion of the Historians, their shining roofs of blue, green, scarlet and lemon-yellow majolica all glinting amid the sacred woods surrounding them.

My eager eyes devoured each and every one of those monuments to Asian antiquity, curious to know more about the inscrutable classes who inhabited them, to know how the institutions had begun, to understand the meaning of their rituals, the spirit behind their literature, their grammar, their dogma, the strange inner workings of the brain of a learned Chinaman . . . But that whole world is inviolable as a sanctuary.

I sat down on the wall, my gaze lost in the sandy plain stretching beyond the gates as far as the foothills of the Mongolian mountains, where endless dustclouds swirl and slow caravans of travellers fill the paths at every hour, day or night. My soul was filled with a melancholy that the lofty silence enfolding Peking transmuted into a more desolate emptiness. It was like a nostalgia for myself, a long-drawn-out grief at finding myself there alone, absorbed into that harsh, barbarous world. With tear-filled eyes, I recalled my village in Minho with its churchyard shaded by oaktrees, the wineshop with the branch of laurel nailed above the door, the blacksmith's shed and the little streams so cool in the season when the flax grows green.

It was the time of year when the doves migrate south from Peking. I saw them gathering in flocks above me, leaving the woods around the temples and the imperial pavilions. To frighten away birds of prey, each one carried a light tube of bamboo through which the wind whistled. The white clouds of birds passed over as if driven by a tender breeze, leaving behind them in the silence a slow, melancholy sigh, an aeolian tremor, that faded slowly upon the pale air.

I returned home feeling troubled and pensive.

At supper, Camilloff unfolded his napkin and asked me cheerily for my impressions of Peking.

'Having seen Peking, General, I now understand the words penned by a poet of ours:

By the rivers that flow through Babylon
I found myself alone . . .'

'Peking *is* something of a monster!' said Camilloff, nodding his bald head thoughtfully. 'And when you think that three hundred million men, a wily, hardworking, long-suffering, prolific and aggressive race, are all ruled by this city and by the conquering Tartar race that runs it. They study our sciences . . . a glass of Médoc, Teodoro? . . . they have a formidable navy, and the army that once believed it could destroy the foreigner with paper dragons breathing snakes of fire now uses Prussian tactics and rifles! It's truly terrifying!'

'And yet in my country, General, when they speak of the Celestial Empire with regard to Macao, our patriots smooth back their hair and say nonchalantly: Fifty or so men should be enough to send the Chinese packing.'

The arrant stupidity of this remark was received in silence. Then the General cleared his throat ostentatiously and murmured diplomatically:

'But Portugal's a fine country . . .'

I exclaimed bluntly and firmly:

'It's a complete mess, General!'

The General's wife, placing a chicken wing delicately on the edge of her plate and wiping her little finger, said:

'But it's the land of the song of Mignon. It is there that the orange tree blooms . . .'

Plump Meriskoff, a German doctor from the University of Bonn, a chancellor at the Legation and a man of poetry and opinions, observed respectfully:

'Madam, the sweet land of Mignon is Italy: Do you know that fortunate land where the orange tree flowers? The divine Goethe was referring to Italy, *Italia mater* . . . which will always be the true beloved of all sensitive souls!'

'I prefer France!' sighed the first secretary's wife, a little freckled doll of a woman with reddish hair.

'Ah, France!' murmured an attaché, rolling huge, moist eyes. Plump Meriskoff adjusted his gold-rimmed spectacles:

'The problem with France, of course, is the Social Question!'

'Oh, the Social Question!' Camilloff grunted darkly.

'Ah, the Social Question!' rumbled the attaché thoughtfully.

And so we talked on in the same wise vein until, at last, it was time for coffee.

As we went out into the garden, the General's wife, leaning sentimentally on my arm, put her face close to mine and murmured:

'What I'd give to live in one of those passionate countries and see the orange trees come into leaf!'

'That, dear lady, is where people really know how to love!' I whispered, leading her gently into the shadows beneath the sycamores.

5

It took one long summer to find out in which province the late Ti Chin-Fu had lived.

This whole administrative saga struck me as both picturesque and quintessentially Chinese! The ever-helpful Camilloff, who would spend whole days trailing from one State office to another, had first to prove that his desire to know the whereabouts of the old Mandarin was not a cover for some plot against the security of the Empire and he further had to swear that his curiosity did not disguise an attack on the sacred rites! Once satisfied with Camilloff's replies, Prince Tong at last allowed an imperial inquiry to be set in motion: the bloom faded from the cheeks of hundreds of scribes as, brush in hand, they toiled day and night over reports set out on rice paper; the offices of the Imperial City, from the Astronomy Tribunal to the Palace of Preferred Benevolence, were filled with the incessant murmur of mysterious conversations; a throng of coolies ran from the Russian Legation to the pavilions of the Forbidden City and from there to the Court of Archives bearing stretchers that groaned beneath the weight of piles of ancient documents.

When Camilloff asked if they had discovered anything, he would receive the satisfying response that they were consulting the Sacred Books of Lao-tzu or that they were about to examine some old texts from the time of Nor Ha-Chu. And to appease the Russian's military impatience, these enigmatic messages from Prince Tong would always be accompanied by a large gift of stuffed sweetmeats or bamboo shoots in sugar syrup.

While the General worked eagerly to find the Ti Chin-Fu family, I sat at his wife's tiny feet weaving hours of silk and gold (to use the words of a Japanese poet).

There was a pavilion in the garden, beneath the sycamores, which was called, in the Chinese fashion, the Pavilion of Discreet Repose. A cool stream sang sweetly as it ran along beside it, flowing under a rustic, pink-painted bridge. The walls were made of fine woven bamboo lined with dark blue silk and when the sun shone through them it filled the interior with a supernatural light of faintest opal. In the middle was a plump divan upholstered in white silk, like a poem of morning cloud, as tempting as a nuptial bed. In each corner stood magnificent translucent jars dating from the Yeng dynasty, filled with the aristocratic elegance of scarlet lilies from Japan. The floor was covered by fine mats from Nanking and, next to the latticework window, on a graceful sandalwood pedestal, a fan made out of strips of glass caught the entering breeze, producing a tender, melancholy note.

Late August mornings in Peking are very sweet. A gentle hint of autumn already drifts upon the air. At that hour Chancellor Meriskoff and the Legation officials were always at the Chancery preparing the diplomatic bag to be sent off to St Petersburg.

At that hour, fan in hand, I would tiptoe along the airy garden paths in my satin slippers, push open the door of the Pavilion of Discreet Repose and call:

'Mimi?'

And, soft as a kiss, the voice of the General's wife would reply:

'Yes?'

How lovely she looked dressed like a Chinese lady! Pale peach blossom bloomed in her hair, which she wore piled high on her head, and her eyebrows, with the help of dye from Nanking, seemed purer and blacker. Her gauze petticoat edged with embroidered gold filigree clung to her small, firm breasts. Her loose foulard trousers, pale as a nymph's thigh, that fell in folds about her slender ankles and her yellow silk stockings, gave her the graceful look of a figure in a seraglio. Her feet were so small I could fit only three fingers of my hand into her tiny slipper.

Her name was Vladimira. She was born near Nizhni Novgorod and had been brought up by an old aunt who admired Rousseau, read *Les Amours du Chevalier de Faublas*, wore her hair powdered and looked like a grotesque Cossack lithograph of a courtly Versailles lady.

Vladimira's dream was to live in Paris and, while she delicately prepared the tea, she would beg me to tell her risqué stories about Parisian ladies of the night and speak to me of her veneration for Dumas *fils*.

I would roll up one long sleeve of her short, russet-coloured jacket and my devoted lips would travel the cool skin of her beautiful arms. Later, lying in dumb ecstasy on the divan, breast to breast, our arms about each other, we would listen to the aeolian music of the glass fan, to the blue-winged magpies fluttering in the plane trees, to the fugitive rhythms of the stream flowing nearby.

Occasionally our eyes, moist with emotion, would alight on the picture hanging above the divan. It was made from black satin and bore maxims in Chinese characters drawn from the Sacred Book of Li-Nun 'concerning wifely duties'. Fortunately, neither of us understood Chinese and, in the silence, our kisses would begin again, long, tender kisses, comparable (to use the florid language of that country) to pearls falling one by one into a silver bowl. Where are they now, those sweet afternoons spent in the gardens of Peking? Where are the dead leaves of those scarlet lilies from Japan?

One morning, Camilloff came into the Chancery where I was smoking the pipe of peace with Meriskoff. He threw down his mighty sabre on a couch and gleefully told us the news given him by the perspicacious Prince Tong.

'It seems that a wealthy Mandarin by the name of Ti Chin-Fu used to live within the frontiers of Mongolia, in the town of Tien-Hó. He died very suddenly and his vast family live on there in poverty in a squalid hovel.'

The discovery had not, in fact, come about thanks to the wisdom of the imperial bureaucrats; it was made by an astrologer in the Temple of Faqua, who had spent twenty nights leafing through the luminous archives of the stars in the heavens above.

'Teodoro, that must be your man!' exclaimed Camilloff.

And Meriskoff, tapping out the ash from his pipe, echoed the same sentiment:

'That must be your man, Teodoro!'

'My man!' I muttered sombrely.

He probably was 'my man' but I was not at all keen on the idea of looking for 'my man' or for his family or embarking on a monotonous trek through the desolate outer limits of China! Moreover, since arriving in Peking, I had not once laid eyes on the hateful form of Ti Chin-Fu and his kite. My conscience lay within me like a sleeping dove. The enormous effort involved in dragging myself away from the sweet temptations of the boulevard and my palace on Largo do Loreto, of having ploughed the seas all the way to the Middle Kingdom, had obviously struck Eternal Justice as being sufficient in itself as both expiation and penitential pilgrimage. Clearly Ti Chin-Fu had calmed down and withdrawn, together with his kite, into a state of everlasting immobility. What was the point then of going to Tien-Hó? Why not stay in the delightful city of Peking, eating water lilies in sugar syrup, abandoning myself to afternoons of amorous somnolence in the Pavilion of Discreet Repose and to blue evenings spent walking arm in arm with good-hearted Dr Meriskoff along the jasper terraces of the Sanctuary of Purification or beneath the cedars of the Temple of Heaven?

But Camilloff, with pen in hand, was already eagerly tracing my route to Tien-Hó on the map, pointing out to me, in unpleasantly close proximity, the shadows of mountains, the tortuous courses of rivers, the dim outlines of lakes.

'Here it is!' he said. 'You travel up as far as Ni Ku-Hé, on the banks of the Pei-Hó. From there you travel in flat-bottomed boats to My-Yun, an excellent city, they even have a living Buddha . . . From there, you'll continue on horseback to the fortress of Ché-Hia and past that most famous of landmarks, the Great Wall! You rest at the fort of Ku Pi-Hó where you can hunt gazelles, wonderful gazelles. And after just a two-day walk you reach Tien-Hó. Brilliant, eh? When do you want to leave? Tomorrow?'

'Tomorrow?' I groaned glumly.

Poor Vladimira! That night, while Meriskoff played his obligatory game of whist with three embassy officials on the other side of the room, and Camilloff sat in one corner of the sofa dozing, with his mouth open and his arms crossed, looking as solemn as if seated on a bench at the Congress of Vienna, she sat down at the piano. By her side, in a pose worthy of a Byronic hero devastated by fate, I lugubriously twirled my moustaches. The sweet creature played just two notes of penetrating sweetness and then began to sing, looking up at me with shining eyes, moist with tears:

> *L'oiseau s'envole,*
> *Là bas, là bas!*
> *L'oiseau s'envole . . .*
> *Ne revient pas . . .*

'This bird *will* return to the nest,' I murmured tenderly and then to hide my tears, I left her, muttering furiously:

'Damn you, Ti Chin-Fu! It's all your fault! You old rascal! You old mischief-maker!'

The next day I set off for Tien-Hó with my respectful interpreter Sá-Tó, a long caravan of carts, two Cossacks and a throng of coolies.

Leaving the wall of the Tartar City behind us, we travelled for a long time past the sacred gardens that border the Temple of Confucius.

It was the end of Autumn. The leaves were already yellow. A poignant sweetness hung in the air. From the holy pavilions came a murmur of hymns, monotonous and sad. Along the terraces slithered huge snakes, venerable as gods, already grown sluggish with the cold. And here and there, as we passed, we saw ancient Buddhists, their skin dry as parchment, limbs gnarled as roots, sitting crosslegged beneath the sycamores, as still as idols, endlessly contemplating their navels, awaiting the perfection of Nirvana.

And I was thinking, as I rode along, with a sadness as pale as that same Asiatic October sky, of the two round tears I had seen shining in Mimi's green eyes when we said goodbye.

6

It was already late evening when we reached Tien-Hó and the sun, red as a shield of molten metal, was sinking fast.

To the south of Tien-Hó, near a torrent loudly tumbling over rocks, rise the black city walls. To the east, the pale, dusty plain stretches as far as a group of dark hills where a white building, a Catholic mission, can be seen. Beyond that, to the distant north, are the eternal purple mountains of Mongolia, hanging in the air like clouds.

We lodged in a stinking shack called the Inn of Earthly Consolation. I was given the best room, which opened out onto a gallery built on wooden stilts. It was strangely ornamented with dragons cut out of paper and suspended on strings from the roof beams. The slightest breeze set this legion of fabulous monsters swaying rhythmically, with the dry rustle of leaves, as if possessed by some grotesque form of supernatural life.

Before it grew dark, I went with Sá-Tó to visit the town, but I soon fled the terrible stench of its alleyways. Everything about it seemed black to me: the hovels, the muddy ground, the fetid water running down its streets, the starving dogs, its miserable inhabitants. I withdrew to the inn where Mongol muleteers and lice-infested children watched me in astonishment.

'Every one of them looks suspicious to me, Sá-Tó,' I said, frowning.

'You're quite right, sir. They're a real rabble. But there's no danger. Before leaving Peking, I killed a black cockerel to placate the goddess Kaonine. So you can go to sleep safe from evil spirits. Would you like some tea, sir?'

'Yes, Sá-Tó, I would.'

Once we'd drunk our tea, we talked about our 'grand plan'. The following morning I was to be the bringer of happiness to the sad hovel in which Ti Chin-Fu's widow lived. I was to tell her of the millions I was going to give her and which I had already deposited in Peking. Then, with the agreement of the ruling Mandarin, we would distribute large quantities of rice to the populace and at night there would be a kind of public gala with coloured lights and dancing.

'What do you think, Sá-Tó?'

'The wisdom of Confucius lives on in your words, sir. It will be wonderful, wonderful!'

Weary from the journey, I soon began to yawn and so stretched myself out on the platform of heated bricks that serves as a bed in Chinese inns. Wrapped in my fur-lined cloak, I made the sign of the cross and went to sleep thinking of Mimi's white arms, of her siren-green eyes.

Around midnight I was awoken by a slow, dull rumbling that surrounded the inn like the sound of a strong wind blowing through a wood, or of heavy waves pounding a sea wall. Moonlight flooded into the room from the open gallery, the sad moonlight of the Asian autumn, lending odd, chimerical shapes to the dragons hanging from the ceiling.

Worried, I sat up, and at that moment a tall, restless figure appeared in the luminous strip of moonlight.

'It's me, sir!' whispered the terrified voice of Sá-Tó and, squatting down next to me, he poured out his fears in a hoarse torrent of words. Whilst I had slept, a rumour had gone round that a stranger, a Foreign Devil, had arrived in town accompanied by trunks crammed with treasure. Ever since nightfall, Sá-Tó had begun noticing sharp faces with greedy eyes circling the inn like impatient jackals. He had at once ordered the coolies to barricade the door with the carts, forming a defensive semicircle, the way the Tartars used to do. But, gradually, the crowd had grown. He had just that minute looked through a spyhole and it seemed the inn was surrounded by the whole population of Tien-Hó, snarling menacingly. The goddess Kaonine had clearly not been satisfied with the blood of one black cockerel. Worse than that, he had earlier seen a black she-goat refuse to enter a pagoda. It would be a night of terrors. And his poor wife, 'bone of his bone', was far, far away in Peking.

'What shall we do now, Sá-Tó?' I asked.

'Now, sir . . . Now . . .'

He fell silent and his thin body trembled, like a dog cringing before the whip.

I pushed the coward away and walked across to the gallery. I looked down. The porch roof attached to the wall opposite cast a deep, dark shadow. A black horde was indeed huddled together there. A figure would sometimes crawl out into the brightness, peering and sniffing at the carts until, feeling the moonlight on his face, he would quickly withdraw, disappearing back into the darkness where I occasionally caught sight of the glinting blade of a lance being lowered to avoid the porch roof.

'What do you want, you dogs?' I yelled.

In response to the sound of this foreign voice, a grunt issued from the darkness and a stone flew past me, crashing through the wax paper of the shutter. Immediately afterwards an arrow whistled by me and fixed itself in a beam just above my head.

I ran down to the kitchen. My coolies were sitting on their heels, their teeth chattering with terror. The two Cossacks accompanying me were sitting impassively by the fire, smoking their pipes, sabres drawn and ready on their knees.

Everyone else, the old bespectacled innkeeper, the ragged old woman I had seen earlier in the courtyard flying a paper kite, the Mongol muleteers and the lice-ridden children had disappeared. Only one old man remained, too befuddled by opium to move. He sat crumpled in a corner like a bundle of rags. Outside I could hear the howling of the mob.

I turned to Sá-Tó, who was leaning against a beam, almost swooning with fear. We had no weapons and the two Cossacks could not possibly repel the attack alone. Someone would have to go and wake the ruling Mandarin and inform him that I was a friend of Camilloff's, a guest of Prince Tong's, and urge him to come and disperse the mob, to uphold the sacred law of hospitality!

But Sá-Tó confessed to me, in a voice as soft as a whisper, that it was almost certainly the governor who was leading the assault! Word of my wealth and some tale about carts laden with gold had inflamed everyone's appetite from the highest authorities down to the poorest beggar! Prudence demanded, with the force of a holy commandment, that we give up part of the treasure, the mules and the boxes of food.

'And stay in this wretched village with no clothes, no money and no provisions?'

'Yes, but with our lives intact, sir!'

I gave in and told Sá-Tó to go and tell the mob that we would make a generous distribution of money on the understanding that they would then return to their houses and respect us as if we were the guests sent by Buddha.

Trembling, Sá-Tó went out onto the balcony and began haranguing the crowd, waving his arms and barking out words. I had already opened a small trunk and was passing up to him rolls and bags of money that he hurled out in fistfuls as if he were sowing seed. From below came the sounds made by the furious rabble as the coins rained down on them. Then came the slow sigh of satisfied greed followed by a silence, the pause of someone expecting more.

'More!' muttered Sá-Tó, turning round anxiously.

Indignantly I gave him more rolls, bags and strings of half-*real* coins threaded together. The trunk was already empty. The still unsatisfied crowd roared.

'More, sir!' begged Sá-Tó.

'I haven't got any more, man! The rest is in Peking!'

'Oh, holy Buddha, then we are lost, lost!' wailed Sá-Tó, falling to his knees.

The rabble, silent now, was still waiting. Suddenly wild ululations rent the air and I heard the eager masses hurl themselves upon the carts arranged in a semicircle around the gate. The timberwork of the Inn of Earthly Consolation groaned and trembled beneath the impact.

I ran to the balcony. Down below I saw a desperate mob encircling the overturned carts. Axes gleamed as they fell on the lids of crates; the leather on the trunks was ripped open by innumerable knives; on the porch the Cossacks were bellowing at each other over who should have the cleaver. Beneath the porch, even in the brilliant moonlight, I could make out the flames of torches giving off clouds of sparks. A hoarse cry arose and, in response, the dogs howled far off in the distance and then, from every alleyway, there emerged running figures and light shadows waving rudimentary spears and scythes.

All of a sudden, I heard the sound of the tumultuous mob pouring in through the splintered doors of the shop downstairs. They were, of course, looking for me, imagining that I would have kept the best of the treasure, precious stones and gold about my person. Crazed with terror, I ran towards a bamboo screen to one side of the courtyard. I knocked it down and jumped over a layer of thick vegetation rank with the sour smell of ordure. My pony, hitched to a crossbar, neighed and pulled furiously at its halter. I hurled myself onto its back and clung on to its mane.

At that moment, the battered kitchen door finally gave way and, with a wild shout, in rushed a horde bearing lanterns and spears. Terrified, the pony jumped a ditch. An arrow whistled past me, then a brick struck me on the shoulder, another in the small of my back, another the pony's haunch, another larger one grazed my ear! Desperately clutching the pony's mane, my chest heaving, my tongue lolling and blood dripping from my ear, I rode off at a furious pace down a pitchblack street. Then I saw before me the city wall, the battlements, the gate to the closed town!

Mad with fear and beyond all human help, with the crowd roaring at my heels, I needed God! I believed in Him, I cried out to Him to save me, and my spirit went into a tumult of ecstasy, offering up to Him any fragments of prayers and Hail Marys that still lingered in the depths of my memory. I turned to look back over the pony's haunches. Around a distant corner appeared a blaze of torches: the rabble! I galloped off beneath the high wall that ran beside me like a vast, black ribbon furiously unravelling. All at once, I spotted a breach in the wall, a huge gap bristling with brambles, on the other side of which lay the moonlit plain, like a vast sheet of sleeping water! I headed desperately in that direction, buffeted about by my prancing pony, and for a long time I galloped hard across the open plain.

Then, suddenly, the pony and I both fell with a dull thud. We were in a lake. Putrid water rushed into my mouth, and my feet became entangled in the soft roots of waterlilies. When I stood up, my feet touched bottom and I could see the pony running, stirrups flying in the wind, already far off, like a shadow.

I began to walk through that wilderness, plunging into mud, trudging through thorny undergrowth. The blood from my ear was still dripping onto my shoulder. In the harsh cold, my sodden clothes froze on my skin, and sometimes I imagined I saw the eyes of wild animals gleaming in the shadows.

At last, I came across an area full of scattered stones on which, beneath a low, black tree, lay one of those piles of yellow coffins that the Chinese leave in the fields, where bodies are left to rot. Exhausted, I collapsed on top of one of the coffins but a terrible stench filled the air and where I had rested my hands on the wood, I felt the viscous touch of the liquid oozing out between the planks. I wanted to run away, but my trembling knees refused to budge and then trees, rocks, tall grasses, the whole horizon began to turn like a spinning disc. Blood-red spots flickered before my eyes and I felt as if I were falling very slowly from a great height, like a feather floating to the ground.

When I came to, I was stretched out on a stone bench in the courtyard of a vast building resembling a monastery and which was wrapped in a profound silence. Two Lazarist fathers were carefully bathing my ear. A cool breeze was blowing, the pulley on a well creaked slowly and a bell tolled for matins. I looked up and saw a white façade with small barred windows and a cross on the roof and, seeing in the peace of that Catholic cloister a corner of my own homeland regained, seeing in it a shelter and a consolation, two silent tears rolled down my cheeks.

7

The two Lazarist fathers had been heading in the direction of Tien-Hó, when they found me at dawn lying unconscious on the road. And, as jovial Father Loriot pointed out, 'not before time', for a black semicircle of those great, lugubrious Tartary crows were gathering around my motionless body, studying me with greedy eyes.

The fathers made a stretcher for me and carried me to the monastery without further delay. There was much rejoicing in the community when they discovered that I was not only a fellow Latin, but a Christian and a subject of Their Most Faithful Majesties.

The monastery formed the centre of a small Catholic village that clustered round the massive edifice like the houses of serfs about a feudal castle. It had been in existence ever since the first missionaries went to Manchuria. We were still within the borders of China there, but beyond lay Mongolia, the Land of Grasses, made up of immense dark-green meadows and endless marshlands, sprinkled with the vivid colours of wild flowers.

There lay the vast plain of the nomads. From my window I could see the dark circles of tents covered in felt or goatskins and sometimes I would watch the departure of a tribe, leading their flocks westwards in a long caravan.

The Lazarist superior was the excellent Father Giulio. His many years spent amongst the yellow-skinned races had almost made a Chinaman of him. When I saw him in the cloister in his purple tunic, long pigtail and venerable beard, cooling himself with a huge fan, he looked to me like some wise and learned Mandarin in the peace of a temple, making mental notes to himself on the Sacred Book of Chu. He was a real saint, but the smell of garlic on his breath would have seen off even the most troubled of souls in need of consolation.

I have very sweet memories of the days I spent there. My room, with its whitewashed walls adorned only by a black cross, had the tranquil modesty of a cell. I would wake when matins was rung and, out of respect for the old missionaries, I would go and hear mass in the chapel. In the clear light of morning, in those Mongolian lands so far from his Catholic homeland, it was touching to see the priest, wearing a chasuble embroidered with a cross, bowing before the altar and to hear his murmured *Dominus vobiscum* and *Cum spiritu tuo* filling the cool silence.

In the afternoon I would visit the school and marvel at the sight of little Chinese children declining *hora, horae* and, after refectory, I would stroll in the cloister and hear stories about distant missions, apostolic journeys to the Land of Meadows, the prison sentences endured, the long marches, the dangers, the heroic chronicles of the Faith.

I, on the other hand, did not tell the monastery's inhabitants the tale of my own fantastic adventures. I passed myself off as an inquisitive tourist, travelling through the world taking notes. And while I waited for my wounded ear to heal, I surrendered myself, with a certain lassitude of spirit, to the peace of the place.

But I was determined, as soon as possible, to leave China, that barbarous Empire I now so thoroughly loathed.

Whenever I remembered how I had come from the farthest corners of the Western World to bring my copious wealth to some Chinese province only to be robbed, stoned and have arrows shot at me the minute I arrived, I was filled by a deep rancour. I spent hours pacing up and down my room, inventing acts of cruelty with which to avenge myself on the Middle Kingdom!

To depart with all my millions was the most practical and easiest act of vengeance. Moreover, my idea of artificially resuscitating the personality of Ti Chin-Fu for the good of China now struck me as absurd, as foolish as a dream. I did not understand the language. I knew nothing of the customs, rites and laws nor of the wise men of that land. What had I come there to do then except expose myself, with my display of

72

wealth, to assaults from a people who for forty-four centuries had been pirates and plunderers both on land and sea?

Besides, Ti Chin-Fu and his kite were still nowhere to be seen, gone no doubt to the Chinese heaven of the Ancestors, and the mitigation of that visible cause of remorse had considerably diminished my desire for expiation.

No doubt the old scholar had grown weary of having to leave the ineffable regions in order to come and lie on my furniture. He had seen the efforts I had made, my desire to be useful to his offspring, his province and his race and, satisfied, had settled down at last to sleep out his eternal siesta. I would never again see his yellow paunch!

And then I would be pricked by the longing to enjoy my wealth in peace, untroubled and free, at my palace on Largo do Loreto or along the boulevard, sipping the honey of the flowers of civilization.

But what of Ti Chin-Fu's widow, his sons' spoiled wives, his little grandchildren? Could I be so cruel as to leave them cold and hungry in the dark alleyways of Tien-Hó? No. They were not to blame for the stones thrown by the rabble. And, as a Christian, having found asylum in a Christian monastery, with the Gospels at my bedside and surrounded by lives that were the very embodiment of Charity, I could not leave the Middle Kingdom without restoring to those whom I had stripped of wealth that honest comfort recommended in Confucius' classic work on Filial Piety.

So I wrote to Camilloff. I told him of my abject flight beneath a hail of stones thrown by a Chinese mob, of the Christian shelter the mission had given me and of my intense desire to leave China. I asked him to send to the widow of Ti Chin-Fu the millions I had deposited in the house of the merchant Tsing-Fó, on the Avenue Chá-Cua, near the triumphal arch of Tong, next to the temple of the goddess Kaonine.

Jovial Father Loriot was off to Peking on a mission and he took with him my letter bearing the monastery seal (a cross emerging from a heart in flames).

The days passed. The first snows gleamed white on the

northern mountains of Manchuria and I spent my time in that Land of Grasses hunting gazelle: intense, invigorating mornings when I would set off at full gallop through the vast, wild air of the plain, accompanied by Mongolian huntsmen emitting vibrant, ululating cries and beating the undergrowth with their spears. Sometimes a gazelle would leap forth and run like the wind, her delicate ears flat against her head. Then we would release the falcon. It would hover on still wings above the gazelle, repeatedly pecking hard, with all the force of its curved beak, at the creature's skull. We would track her down at last to the bank of some stagnant pool covered with waterlilies. Then the black dogs of Tartary would scramble onto her belly and stand with their paws in her blood, their sharp teeth slowly unravelling her entrails.

Finally, one morning, the layman at the main gate spotted Father Loriot galloping back in great haste up the steep hill to the village, his knapsack on his back and a small child in his arms. He had found her abandoned, naked and dying by the side of the road. He had immediately baptized her in a nearby stream and given her the name 'Well-Found'. He was tenderness itself to the girl and arrived out of breath in his haste to reach the convent and give the starving child some of their excellent goat's milk.

After embracing the other friars and mopping the fat beads of sweat from his brow, he drew from his breeches pocket an envelope bearing the seal of the Russian eagle.

'This is from old Camilloff, friend Teodoro. He's in excellent health, as is his wife. In fine fettle, both of them.'

I ran to a corner of the cloister in order to read the two-page letter. My good friend Camilloff, with his bald head and owlish eyes, had a truly original way of combining the common sense of a skilled chancellor and the picaresque bickerings of a burlesque diplomat. The letter read as follows:

Friend, guest and dearest Teodoro,
    The first few lines of your letter had us worried but, as we read on, it was with great relief that we learned you were with the holy fathers in their Christian mission. I went at once to the imperial

*office to lodge a serious complaint with Prince Tong regarding the
Tien-Hó scandal. His Excellency expressed extravagant joy at
the news. For while, as a private individual, he regrets the attack,
the theft and the stoning suffered by my guest, as a minister of the
Empire he sees in all this a heaven-sent opportunity to extract from
the town of Tien-Hó, as punishment for injury done to a foreigner,
a fine amounting to the handsome sum of three hundred thousand
francs or, according to the calculations of our wise friend Meriskoff,
fifty-four* contos de réis *in the currency of your own splendid country! It is, as Meriskoff said, an excellent result both for the imperial
Exchequer and for your ear, which thus stands copiously revenged.
It's beginning to turn cold here and we're all in our fur coats
already. The worthy Meriskoff is suffering with his liver, but the
pain has diminished neither his philosophical faculties nor his wise
eloquence. We have suffered a great sadness: on the morning of the
fifteenth, the little dog, the adorable Tu-Tu, that belonged to the
excellent Madame Tagarieff, the wife of our dear secretary, disappeared. I went straight to the police, but Tu-Tu has not been
returned and our sorrow is only made worse by the knowledge that
the Peking hoi poloi consider such small dogs, stewed in sugar
syrup, to be a delicacy. Another really terrible thing happened
and one that brought with it disastrous consequences. At the last
Legation supper, the French minister's wife, that rude woman
Madame Grijon, that 'dry old stick' (as our Meriskoff calls her),
contravened all the international rules of etiquette by offering both
her arm, her scrawny arm, and the place to her right at table to a
mere British attaché, Lord Gordon! What do you say to that?
Can you credit it? Is it rational? It spells the end of the social order!
Giving her arm and the place to her right at table to an attaché – a
Scotsman with a face as red as a tomato and a monocle always
glued in one eye – in front of everyone, ambassadors, ministers and
myself! I can't begin to tell you the sensation this has caused in the
diplomatic corps. We await instructions from our governments. As
Meriskoff said, with a sad shake of his head: this is serious, very
serious indeed! It proves (and no one doubts it) that Lord Gordon
is the dry old stick's 'favourite son'. What corruption! What
depravity! My wife has not been well since your departure for the
wretched city of Tien-Hó. Dr Pagloff can find nothing wrong with*

her. She suffers from listlessness, lassitude, a kind of nostalgic indolence that prostrates her for hours at a time on the sofa in the Pavilion of Discreet Repose, an absent look in her eyes, a sigh on her lips. I'm not so easily fooled. I know exactly what it is that troubles her: it's that awful bladder infection she picked up from the bad water we drank at the Legation in Madrid. May God's will be done . . . She asked me to send you 'un petit bonjour' and requests that as soon as you reach Paris, if you go to Paris that is, you send by diplomatic bag to St Petersburg (from there it will be forwarded to Peking), two dozen twelve-button gloves, size five and three quarters, made by 'Sol', from the Magasins du Louvre, as well as the latest novels by Zola, Mademoiselle de Maupin *by* Gautier *and a box of 'Opoponax' . . . Oh, and I forgot to tell you that we've changed baker's. The bakery at the British embassy supplies us now. We left the one at the French embassy in order to have no further dealings with the 'dry old stick' . . . It demonstrates yet again the inconvenience of not having our own bakery here in the Russian embassy, despite all the reports and petitions I've despatched on the matter to the Chancery at St Petersburg! They know perfectly well that there are no bakeries in Peking, that each legation has its own, as a symbol of both permanence and influence. But what happens? The imperial court simply ignores the highest interests of Russian civilization! . . . I think that's all the news from Peking and the legations. Meriskoff sends his regards as does everyone at the embassy; also young Count Arthur, Zizi from the Spanish embassy, 'Sourpuss' and Lulu; in short everyone, especially me.*

Affectionately yours,
General Camilloff

PS In respect of the widow of the family of Ti Chin-Fu, a mistake was made. The astrologer in the temple of Faqua got his sidereal interpretations wrong. That particular family does not in fact live in Tien-Hó. They live in the south of China, in the province of Canton. Although there is another Ti Chin-Fu family living beyond the Great Wall, almost on the Russian border, in the district of Kao-Li. In both cases the head of the household has died

leaving the families in dire poverty. I have not, therefore, with-
drawn the money from the house of Tsing-Fó and I await further
instructions. This new information was sent to me today by His
Excellency Prince Tong, together with a delicious calabash jam
. . . I'm pleased to tell you too that Sá-Tó got back safely from
Tien-Hó, with a split lip and a few slight bruises to his shoulder,
having managed to salvage from the luggage only a lithograph of
Our Lady of Sorrows, which I see, from the inscription in ink,
belonged to your worthy mother . . . My valiant Cossacks, alas,
remained there in a pool of blood. His Excellency Prince Tong has
agreed to pay me ten thousand francs per Cossack out of the money
he extracts from the town of Tien-Hó. Sá-Tó tells me that if, as is
only natural, you should wish to recommence your travels across the
Empire in search of the Ti Chin-Fu family, he would consider
himself both fortunate and honoured to accompany you, with
dog-like fidelity and Cossack docility.
    Camilloff

'No, never!' I roared out loud, crumpling up the letter as I
strode up and down the melancholy cloister. 'No, by God or
by the Devil, I won't! Tramp the roads of China again? Never!
What more hideous, ghastly fate! I left the delights of my
palace on Largo do Loreto and my love-nest in Paris, I was
tossed about on turbulent seas all the way from Marseilles to
Shanghai, I put up with fleas on Chinese barges, the stench of
alleyways, the dust of arid roads and for what? I had a plan that
rose up to the Heavens, splendid and ornate as any monument. The whole edifice glittered from top to bottom with
every kind of good intention and now I see it fall, piece by
piece, to the ground, where it lies in ruins! I wanted to offer
my name, my millions and half my golden bed to a lady of the
Ti Chin-Fu family, but the social prejudices of a barbarous
race would not let me! My ambition, once I had received the
title of Mandarin, was to refashion the destiny of China, to
bring prosperity to its people, but the imperial law forbids it! I
wanted to pour out upon this starving rabble an endless
stream of charity, but I ran the disagreeable risk of being
decapitated as an instigator of rebellions! I came to enrich a

77

town but instead was stoned by the turbulent masses! I came to bestow wealth, the comfort that Confucius himself had praised, on the Ti Chin-Fu family but that family disappeared, evaporated like smoke, and now other Ti Chin-Fu families spring up, some here, some there, in the south, in the west, like diversionary flares. And now I'm expected to go to Canton, to Kao-Li, to expose my other ear to brutal injury by bricks, to flee again across barren plains, clinging to the mane of a horse? No, never again!'

I stopped and, with uplifted arms, addressed the cloister, the trees and the soft, silent air about me:

'Ti Chin-Fu!' I cried. 'Ti Chin-Fu! I did everything that reason, generosity and logic demanded in order to placate you! Venerable sage, tell me, are you, your fine kite and your government official's paunch finally satisfied? Speak to me! Speak to me!'

I listened, I looked. At that noontime hour, there was only the sound of the pulley on the well in the courtyard slowly creaking. Beneath the mulberry trees, along the arches of the cloister, the leaves gathered in the October tea harvest were laid out on silk paper to dry; from the half-open door to the classroom came the slow murmur of Latin declensions; it was a harsh peace, composed of the simplicity of everyday tasks, the honest pleasure of study and the bucolic air of that hill on which, beneath a white winter sun, the religious community slept. And from that serenity all about me, I seemed suddenly to receive into my own soul a sense of absolute peace!

My fingers still trembling, I lit a cigar and then, wiping a drop of sweat from my brow, I spoke these words, the summation of a whole destiny:

'Ti Chin-Fu is satisfied.'

Then I went to Father Giulio's cell, where he was sitting at the window with the monastery cat on his lap, reading his breviary and nibbling sugar almonds.

'Most Reverend Father, I'm going back to Europe . . . Is one of your good friars by any chance going on a mission to Shanghai or thereabouts?'

The venerable superior put on his round glasses and, leafing piously through a vast register filled with Chinese characters, he murmured:

'The fifth day of the tenth Moon . . . Yes, Father Anacleto is going to Tientsin for the novena of the Brothers of the Holy Crèche and in the twelfth Moon, Father Sánchez is also going to Tientsin, to give catechism to the orphans there. Yes, dear guest, you shall have companions on your journey east.'

'Tomorrow?'

'Tomorrow. Parting is painful in this part of the world, when souls find understanding in each other through Jesus. Father Gutiérrez will make you up a good food parcel. We already love you like a brother, Teodoro. Do have a sweet, they're delicious. Things rest easy when they find their right place and natural element: the right place for the heart of man is in the heart of God and yours is in that safe place of asylum. Have another sweet . . . But what's this, my son, what's this?'

I was placing a roll of English banknotes on his breviary, which was open at a page on the Evangelical Counsel on Poverty. I stammered out:

'To help the poor, most Reverend Father . . .'

'Excellent, excellent . . . Our good Gutiérrez will make you up a generous food parcel. Amen, my son. *In Deo omnia spes . . .*'

The next day, the bells rang out as I mounted the monastery's white mule and rode down to the village, flanked by Father Anacleto and Father Sánchez. From there we went to Hiang-Ham, a dark, walled town, where they moor the boats that go down to Tientsin. The lands along the Pei-Hó were white with snow and the water was already freezing in the low-lying bays. Bundled up in sheepskins, the good fathers and I sat around the stove in the stern of the boat and spoke about the work of the missionaries, of things Chinese, even, occasionally, about Heavenly matters, all the time passing round a large bottle of gin.

In Tientsin I parted from my two saintly comrades. And two weeks later, at noon on a day of tepid sunshine, I was smoking a cigar and observing the bustle on the Hong Kong docks as I walked the promenade deck of the *Java*, which was about to weigh anchor for Europe.

It was an emotional moment for me, when, with the first turns of the propeller, I saw the lands of China begin to move off into the distance.

From the moment I had woken that morning, a dull disquiet had returned to weigh upon my soul. I recalled that I had come to that vast empire to quell the fearful protests of my conscience with an act of expiation and here I was leaving, driven by my own nervous impatience, having achieved nothing, apart from dishonouring the white moustaches of a brave Russian general and sustaining an injury to my ear after being stoned in a Mongolian border town.

Mine was certainly a strange destiny!

I remained on deck until nightfall, leaning sombrely on the ship's rail, watching the smooth sea, like a vast piece of blue silk, fold at the edges into two soft creases. Large stars gradually began to appear and they hung trembling in the concave darkness whilst, in the shadows below, the propeller turned rhythmically. Then, overtaken by a languorous fatigue, I set to wandering about the ship: the compass, illuminated at night, the piles of winches, the bright clarity of the engine parts all keeping time, the sparks escaping from the funnel in a swirl of black billowing smoke, the red-bearded sailors standing motionless at the rudder and the silhouettes of the pilots on the bridge, tall and indistinct in the dark. In the captain's cabin, an Englishman in a pith helmet, surrounded by ladies drinking cognac, was playing the flute, a melancholy air known as 'Bonnie Dundee'.

It was eleven o'clock when I went down to my berth. The lights were out already, but the round, white moon that had just risen above the water cast one brilliant ray in through the cabin window and there, in that pale half-glow, I saw the paunchy figure stretched out in the hammock, dressed, as always, in yellow silk and clutching his kite to his breast!

It was *him*, again!

And it was him again and again from that moment on! It

was him in Singapore and in Ceylon. It was him rising up from the sands of the desert as we sailed up the Suez Canal; it was him strolling on the prow of a provisions ship when we stopped in Malta; it was him sliding down the slopes of the rosy mountains of Sicily and emerging from the mists surrounding the rock of Gibraltar! And when I disembarked in Lisbon, at the Cais das Colunas, his pot-bellied figure filled the whole archway of Rua Augusta. He fixed me with his slanting eye and even the painted eyes of his kite seemed to be staring at me too.

8

Convinced that I would never be able to placate Ti Chin-Fu, I spent the whole of that night in my room in my palace on the Largo do Loreto, where, as before, the innumerable candles dappled the damask curtains with reds the colour of fresh blood, and I considered how best to rid myself of those supernatural millions, as if I were ridding myself of the trappings of sin. That way I might perhaps free myself once and for all of that paunch and that hateful kite!

I left my palace and gave up my nabob existence. I put on a threadbare jacket and went back to Madame Marques' house. I returned to the office, my spine bent, to beg for my 20 *mil-réis* a month and my beloved quill!

But a greater suffering came to sour my days. Assuming I was bankrupt, all those whom my wealth had once humbled now heaped insults on me, the way people smear with filth the fallen statue of a ruined prince. In a triumph of irony, the newspapers mocked my poverty. The Aristocracy, who had fallen tongue-tied with adulation at the feet of the nabob, now ordered their coachmen to run down in the streets the flinching figure of the ministry scribe. The Clergy, whom I had enriched, accused me of being a 'wizard', the People threw stones at me and, when I complained meekly of the granitic toughness of her steaks, Madame Marques planted her two hands on her hips and shouted:

'Well, what do you expect, Pipsqueak? You'll just have to put up with it! Beggars can't be choosers, you know!'

And despite that act of expiation, old Ti Chin-Fu, fat and yellow as ever, never left my side, since the millions that lay useless and untouched in the banks were still, alas, mine.

At last, indignant at this state of affairs, I made a sudden, ostentatious return to my palace and to my life of luxury. That night, the Largo do Loreto was once more ablaze with the light from my windows and, as before, the great door stood open to reveal long lines of decorative lackeys in their black silk livery.

Immediately, unhesitatingly, all Lisbon threw itself at my feet. Madame Marques wept and called me 'child of her heart'. The newspapers loaded me with epithets normally applied only to the Divinity: I was Omnipotent, Omniscient! The Aristocracy kissed my fingers as they would those of a tyrant and the Clergy wafted me with clouds of incense as if I were an idol. And my scorn for humanity grew so great that it came to include even God, its creator.

After that, an enervating satiety kept me for weeks at a time prostrate on a sofa, silent and morose, contemplating the joy of not-being.

One night, walking back home alone along a deserted street, I saw the Personage all dressed in black and with his umbrella under his arm, the same man who in my happy room in Travessa da Conceição had made me, with the ringing of one small bell, the inheritor of all those hateful millions. I ran over to him, seized him by the lapels of his bourgeois overcoat and yelled:

'Free me from my riches! Bring the Mandarin back to life! Restore to me the peace of poverty!'

He gravely shifted the umbrella to his other arm and said kindly:

'That's not possible, dear sir, not possible at all.'

I threw myself at his feet, in abject supplication, but saw before me, by the dull light of the gaslamps, only the scrawny body of a dog nosing about in the rubbish.

I never found that man again. And now the world seems to me a huge mound of ruins where my soul cries out ceaselessly, in exile amongst the fallen columns.

The flowers in my rooms wither and no one replaces them; the dullest of lights dazzles me as if it were a blazing torch; and when my lovers in their white peignoirs come to lie in my bed, I weep, as if they were the shrouded legions of my dead joys. I sense that I am dying. I have made my will. In it I bequeath my millions to the Devil. They belong to him, let him claim them and share them out.

And to you men I leave, without further comment, these words: 'The only bread that tastes good is the bread we earn day by day with our own hands; never kill the Mandarin!'

And yet, even at the moment of my death, I find immense consolation in this thought: that from north to south and from east to west, from the Great Wall of Tartary to the waves of the Yellow Sea, in the whole vast Empire of China, not one Mandarin would remain alive if you, dear reader, creature improvised by God, a poor creation shaped out of poor clay, my fellow and my brother, if you could snuff him out as easily as I did and thus inherit all his millions!

Angers, June 1880

THE
IDIOSYNCRASIES OF
A YOUNG BLONDE
WOMAN

1

He began by telling me that his story was a simple one . . . and that his name was Macário.

I should first explain that I met this man at a lodging house in Minho. He was tall and well-built; a few sparse white hairs bristled about his smooth, shiny, bald pate, and from behind his round tortoiseshell glasses, his dark eyes – even though they were dark and puffy and the skin about them yellow and wrinkled – gleamed with a singular clarity and rectitude. He was clean-shaven and had a firm, resolute chin. He was wearing a black satin cravat fixed at the back with a buckle, and a long cream-coloured jacket with narrow sleeves and velvet cuffs; the soft folds of an embroidered shirt emerged from beneath his silk waistcoat upon which glinted an antique watch chain.

This happened in September when the days were already growing shorter, and a fine, dry wind chilled the air and the heavy darkness. I had got down from the carriage feeling tired and hungry and I was shivering beneath the scarlet-striped horse blanket I had wrapped about me.

We had just travelled through the tawny, barren landscape of the mountains. It was eight o'clock at night. The skies were dull and overcast. Whether it was a certain cerebral drowsiness brought on by the monotonous swaying of the carriage, or the nervous debility of fatigue, or the influence of the steep plateaux on the hollow night-time silence, or the oppressively thundery atmosphere high up in the hills, the fact was that I, by nature positive and realistic, had been tormented by dreams and imaginings. There is a remnant of mysticism in the depths of all of us, however cool and educated we might be, and sometimes all it takes is a gloomy landscape, or an old cemetery wall, the ascetic solitude of a wilderness, the emollient whiteness of moonlight, for that remnant of mysticism to rise and spread like a mist, filling our soul, our senses and our thoughts; then even the most mathematical and rational of men is apt to become as sad, visionary and idealistic as an old poet-monk. What had plunged me into dreams and chimera was the sight of the Monastery of Rostelo which I had seen in the distance, set on a gentle hill, in the soft, autumnal light of evening. Then, as night was falling and the carriage swayed on in time to the feeble trotting of the scrawny white horses pulling it, and the coachman, his head buried in the hood of his cloak, sat ruminating over his pipe, I began, elegiacally, ridiculously, to consider the sterility of life; I imagined life as a monk in a tranquil monastery set amongst trees or in the murmurous depths of a valley and how, while the water in the valley sang sweetly in its basin of stone, I would read *The Imitation of Christ*, listening to the nightingales in the laurel groves, thinking longingly of heaven. All arrant nonsense, of course. But that was how I felt and I attribute to that visionary mood the interest and feeling stirred up in me by the story told by the man with the velvet cuffs.

My curiosity was first aroused at supper as I was slicing into my breast of chicken served with lashings of white rice and slices of scarlet sausage; the plump, freckled maid was filling my glass with sparkling *vinho verde*, pouring it from high up out of a glass pitcher. The man was sitting opposite me calmly eating a dish of jelly. With my mouth full and holding my linen napkin delicately in my fingertips, I asked him if he was from Vila Real.

'Yes, I've lived there for years,' he said.

'I hear that Vila Real women are very pretty,' I said.

The man said nothing.

'Or don't you agree?' I asked.

The man withdrew into a stiff silence. Up until then, he had been quite happy – laughing, loquacious and full of bonhomie. But then his open smile froze.

I realised that I had re-opened the wound of some memory. Clearly, a woman had played a part in the fate of that old man. Therein lay his personal melodrama or farce, for, unconsciously, I had decided that the man's story would inevitably be grotesque, ridiculous.

So I said to him:

'Someone told me once that the women of Vila Real are the prettiest in the whole of Minho. If you want dark eyes go to Guimarães, if you want a girl with a nice figure go to Santo Aleixo, and for lovely hair, Arcos – apparently the girls there have hair the colour of golden corn.'

The man remained silent, his eyes lowered, and continued eating.

'For slender waists, Viana, for good skin, Amarante, and for all those things together, Vila Real. I have a friend who went to Vila Real to get married. Perhaps you know him. His name's Peixoto, a tall chap with a fair beard, a graduate.'

'Yes, I know Peixoto,' he said, looking at me gravely.

'He went to Vila Real to get married for the same reason that some people used to go to Andalusia: a question of getting the *crème de la crème* of perfection. Your health.'

I was obviously embarrassing him, for he got up and walked with ponderous steps over to the window; that was when I noticed his heavy shoes with their kerseymere uppers, thick soles and leather laces. He left the room.

When I asked for my candle, the maid brought me an ancient brass candlestick and said:

'You're with another gentleman. In room number 3.'

In lodging houses in Minho, a bedroom often turns out to be a cramped dormitory.

'Fine,' I said.

Room number 3 was at the far end of the corridor. Outside the doors on either side the travellers had placed their shoes to be cleaned: there were heavy riding boots all covered in mud, complete with spurs and chains; the white shoes of a hunter; the tall, red boots of a landowner; the high boots of a priest, with their silk tassles; the battered calf-leather ankle boots of a student; and, outside one of the doors, number 15, a pair of women's boots, tiny and slender, with beside them the even tinier lace-up boots of a child, all scuffed and worn, the unlaced legs of the kid boots flopped over to one side.

Everyone was asleep. Outside room number 3 stood the thick-soled boots with the leather laces and when I opened the door, I saw the man with the velvet cuffs. He was wearing a short sprigged jacket, long, thick woollen socks and soft slippers, and was in the process of tying a silk scarf around his head.

'You don't mind, do you?' he asked.

'Feel free,' I said, and to establish a certain intimacy I removed my jacket.

I won't go into the reasons why, shortly after that, when he was already lying down in bed, he started telling me his story, but there's a Slav proverb from Galicia that says: 'What you wouldn't tell your wife or your best friend, tell to a stranger in an inn.' He experienced unexpected, overwhelming rages during his long, sad confession. (It all arose because of my friend, Peixoto, who went to Vila Real to get married.) I saw that man of almost sixty weep. His story may be deemed trivial, but to me that night, with my nerves on edge and feeling generally overwrought, it seemed a most tragic tale. I will relate it, though, as if it were merely an unusual love story.

He began by telling me that his story was a simple one . . . and that his name was Macário.

I asked him then if he was from a family I used to know whose surname was Macário. When he replied that he was a cousin of theirs, I immediately took a liking to him because the Macários were a very old family, a kind of dynasty of merchants, who kept up their old traditions of honesty and scrupulousness with almost religious severity. Macário told me that at the time, in 1823 or 1833 I think he said, in his youth, his Uncle Francisco owned a mercer's shop in Lisbon and he was one of the assistants. The uncle soon noticed Macário's native intelligence, as well as his practical and arithmetical talents, and he put him in charge of the accounts. Macário became his book-keeper.

He told me that, since he was by nature rather lethargic, indeed, even shy, his life at the time was very limited. It consisted of carrying out his work meticulously and faithfully, occasionally lunching in the country and taking unusual care over his clothes and personal linen. His life then was narrow and homely. A very simple social life has a clarifying effect on one's habits; the mind is more ingenuous, feelings less complicated.

A jolly supper sitting beneath the vine trellises in a garden somewhere, watching a stream flowing past, or weeping over the melodramas that were performed by candlelight at the Salitre, these were pleasures enough for a prudent member of the bourgeoisie. Besides, those were confusing and revolutionary times, and there's nothing like a war to make a man more withdrawn, more tied to his hearth, simpler and more easily contented. It is peace which, giving free rein to the imagination, arouses the impatience of desire.

When he was twenty-two years old, Macário had still not been 'tempted by Venus' in the words of an old aunt of his who had been the mistress of Judge Curvo Semedo, a member of that illustrious literary society, the Arcádia.

However, at that point, a woman moved into the third-floor apartment of the building opposite the mercer's shop, a woman of about forty, all dressed in black, with a pale, matte complexion, a pleasingly rounded bust and of a generally desirable appearance. Macário's office was on the first floor above the shop and his desk stood next to a balcony; one morning, he saw that woman come to the window to shake out a dress; she was wearing a white dressing gown that revealed her bare arms, and her black, curly hair hung loose about her shoulders. Macário casually thought to himself that at twenty that woman must have been a captivating and imposing figure; for her thick, coarse hair, her bold eyebrows, her full lips and her firm, aquiline profile spoke of an active temperament and a passionate imagination. Meanwhile, he continued calmly filling up his columns with figures. That night, though, he was sitting smoking at the window of his room, which opened onto the courtyard; it was July and the night air was sensual and electric. A neighbour was playing a tune on a recorder, a Moorish ballad that was popular at the time, a song from a melodrama; the room was immersed in a sweet, mysterious penumbra and, sitting there in his slippers, Macário set to thinking about that thick, black hair and those arms the colour of pale marble. He stretched and rolled his head lazily from side to side against the back of his wicker chair, like a cat scratching itself, and he concluded, yawning, that his life really was very dull. The next day he still felt the same and, sitting down at his desk with the window wide open, gazing across at the building opposite where the woman with the black hair lived, he began languidly sharpening the nib of his quill. No one appeared at the green-framed window. Macário felt irritated, bored, and his work went slowly. He imagined that out in the street the sun would be shining brightly; he thought how sweet it would be to sit in the shade in the countryside and watch white butterflies fluttering around the honeysuckle. When he closed his desk, he heard a window open opposite; it must be the woman with the black hair. Instead a blonde head appeared. Macário immediately went over to the balcony in order to sharpen a pencil. She was a girl of about twenty perhaps, slender, fresh, and as fair as an Englishwoman. The whiteness of her skin had something of the transparency of old porcelain and her profile had a pure line to it, like the profile on an antique medal; picturesque poets of the old school would have used terms such as: dove, ermine, snow and gold to describe her.

Macário said to himself:

'She's the daughter.'

The other woman wore black, but the blonde girl was wearing a muslin dress with blue spots, a chambray scarf tied crossways over her chest and lace cuffs on her sleeves; everything about her was clean, young, fresh, lithe and tender.

In those days Macário also had fair hair and sported a neat beard. His hair was curly, and he doubtless had that thin, rather tense air so common among the plebeian races after the eighteenth century and the Revolution.

Naturally, the girl noticed Macário, but equally naturally, she shut the window and hurriedly drew the embroidered muslin curtain. Those small curtains date from the time of Goethe and they play an intriguing role in romantic life, for they are very revealing. Lifting one corner and peering out, gently creasing it, shows that one is interested; closing the curtain, pinning a flower to it, making it twitch slightly to make quite clear that behind it an attentive face is watching, waiting – these are all ancient ways by which a romance can begin, in both reality and in art. The curtain rose very slowly and a fair-skinned face peered out.

Macário did not go into minute detail about his feelings. He said simply that within five days he was mad about her. His work became slow and inaccurate, and his beautiful italic hand, so clear and firm, acquired curves, hooks and flourishes that revealed all the impatient romance of his nerves. He could not see her in the mornings; the mordant, searing July sun beat down upon the little window. Only in the afternoons would the curtain be pulled back, the window opened and she, placing a pillow on the windowsill, would lean there, looking cool and pretty, fanning herself. The fan worried Macário: it was a round Chinese fan made from white silk delicately embroidered with scarlet dragons; it was edged with blue feathers, fine and tremulous as down; the handle was made of ivory inlaid with mother-of-pearl in the Persian manner and from it hung two golden tassels.

It was a magnificent fan, and it was surprising to find such a fan in the plebeian hands of a girl dressed in simple muslin. However, since she was blonde and her mother dark, Macário, with the intuitive interpretive skills of one in love, said to his curious heart: 'She must be the daughter of an Englishman.' The English go to China, Persia, Hormuz, Australia and return laden down with exotic luxuries like that; even Macário didn't know quite why that Chinese fan pre-occupied him so, but in his own words: 'it caught his fancy'.

A week went by. Then one day from his office window Macário saw the blonde girl go out into the street with her mother – he had grown used to thinking of that splendid person, so magnificently pale and swathed in black, as her mother.

Macário went to the window, saw them cross the road and go into the shop, his shop! He immediately went downstairs, trembling, anxious, passionate, his heart beating furiously. The two women were standing by the counter and an assistant was showing them a roll of black cashmere. This touched Macário. He himself said so.

'Because, after all, dear chap, there was no reason why they should need to buy black cashmere.'

They didn't need it for riding skirts, they certainly wouldn't want to upholster chairs in it, and they had no menfolk at home; that visit to the warehouse was, therefore, a delicate way of seeing him close to, of speaking to him; it had the penetrating charm of a sentimental lie. Were that so, I said to Macário, did he not find that amorous stratagem odd, since it suggested that the mother was in some way an accomplice to it? He confessed to me that the idea had not even occurred to him. Instead, he went over to the counter and remarked foolishly:

'Yes, indeed, you won't find finer cashmere anywhere and it's guaranteed not to shrink.'

And the blonde girl looked at him with her blue eyes and Macário felt as if he were wrapped in all the sweetness of heaven.

Just as he was about to utter some revealing, passionate word, his Uncle Francisco appeared at the back of the shop in his long, cream jacket with the yellow buttons. Since it was not usual to find the book-keeper standing at the counter and since Uncle Francisco, with his narrow, bachelor views, was easily shocked, Macário went slowly back up the spiral staircase to the office, but not before he heard the blonde girl ask sweetly in her delicate voice:

'Could you show me some Indian scarves as well?'

And the cashier went to look for a small package of scarves, bound together with a strip of gold paper.

Macário, who had seen in that visit a confession of love, almost a declaration, spent all day consumed by the bitter impatience of passion. He was childishly distracted and absentminded, unable to concentrate on the accounts; he dined in silence, paying no attention to his Uncle Francisco when the latter praised the meatballs; he barely glanced at the salary he was paid at three o'clock on the dot and gave little heed to his uncle's remarks nor to the shop assistants' concern over the disappearance of a package of Indian scarves.

'That's what happens when you let poor people into the shop,' his Uncle Francisco had pronounced with majestic concision. '12,000 *réis* worth of scarves; put it on my bill.'

Meanwhile, Macário was secretly pondering a letter. The next day, however, whilst he was standing at the balcony, the mother, she of the black hair, appeared at the window and leaned on the sill; at that moment, a friend of Macário's was passing and, seeing the lady, he acknowledged her and took off his straw hat to her, smiling and bowing. Macário was overjoyed. That night he sought out his friend and asked him straight out:

'Who was that woman you greeted today as you were passing the shop?'

'Her name's Senhora Vilaça. A beautiful woman.'

'And what about the daughter?'

'The daughter?'

'Yes, a pale, blonde girl with a Chinese fan.'

'Oh, her. She's the daughter.'

'That's what I said.'

'What about her?'

'She's pretty.'

'She certainly is.'

'And are they respectable people?'

'They are.'

'Good. Do you know them well?'

'I know them, though not well. I used to see them at Dona Claúdia's.'

'Right, now listen.'

Macário recounted the tale of his newly-awoken passion and spoke of his love in the exalted tones of the time, begging his friend, as if his life depended on it, to find 'some way to slip him in'. It wasn't difficult. Each Saturday the Vilaças used to visit the house of a wealthy notary public in Rua dos Calafates: these were quiet, simple gatherings where people would sing motets accompanied by the harpsichord, or play charades and various parlour games from the time of Maria I, and at nine o'clock the maid would serve *horchata*. The very next Saturday, Macário – wearing a blue jacket, cotton trousers with metal straps, and a purple satin cravat – was bowing to the wife of the notary public, Senhora Dona Maria da Graça, a cool, sharp-tempered lady, who was wearing a dress embroidered in many colours, a huge tortoiseshell pince-nez perched on her hooked nose and a marabou feather in her greying hair. In one corner of the room, amidst a rustle of vast dresses, stood the blonde girl, dressed in white, looking as simple and fresh as if she had stepped out of a coloured engraving. Her pale and magnificent mother was gossiping with an apoplectic-looking judge. The notary public was a man of letters, a Latin scholar and a friend of the muses; he wrote in a journal of the time called *The Ladies' Pander*, for he was, above all else, a gallant and even referred to himself in a picturesque ode as 'Venus's pageboy'. Thus the arts were given pride of place at his gatherings and that night a poet of the time was supposed to come and read a short poem entitled: 'Elmira or the Revenge of the Venetian'. That was in the early days of the new audacious romanticism. The revolutions in Greece were beginning to attract romantic spirits steeped in mythology to the marvellous lands of the east. The name of the Pasha of Janina was on everyone's lips. The poetry of the time reveals a voracious appetite for that new, virginal world of minarets, seraglios, sultan's wives with skin the colour of amber, pirates from the archipelago, and ornate, aloe-scented rooms where decrepit pashas lounged about and petted tame lions. People were therefore curious to know more and so, when the poet appeared – with his noble, aquiline nose and his long hair, wearing an old-fashioned tail-coat and clutching the metal tube containing his university diploma – Macário was the only person present to remain entirely unmoved, being completely absorbed in conversation with the young blonde woman. He was saying to her tenderly:

'Did you like those cashmeres you were looking at the other day?'

'Very much,' she said in a low voice.

And from that moment, they were destined for marriage.

Meanwhile, in the large drawing-room, a spiritual time was being had by all. Macário was unable to give all the historical details and characteristics of that gathering. He remembered only that a magistrate from Leiria recited the 'Madrigal to Lydia': he read it standing up, holding a magnifying glass over the page, his right leg slightly forward and one hand gripping the edge of his white waistcoat, while all around him, in a circle, stood the ladies in flower-print dresses decorated with feathers, with narrow sleeves ending in a foam of lace cuff and black lace mittens glittering with rings; they smiled sweetly, gossiped, murmured, giggled and gently fluttered sequinned fans. 'Very nice,' they said, 'very nice indeed.' And the magistrate, setting the magnifying glass to one side, bowed and smiled, revealing one rotten tooth.

Then the lovely Dona Jerónima da Piedade e Sande sat down rather nervously at the harpsichord and in her nasal voice sang that old aria by Sully:

> *Oh Richard, oh my king,*
> *The world is leaving you.*

This provoked the fearsome Gaudêncio, a democrat from the 1820s and an admirer of Robespierre, to snarl bitterly to Macário:

'Kings – they're all snakes the lot of them!'

Then Canon Saavedra sang a popular song from Pernambuco often sung in the time of King João VI and entitled: 'Pretty girls, pretty girls.' And so the night passed, literary, leisurely, erudite, cultured and buzzing with muses.

Eight days later, on a Sunday, Macário was received into the Vilaça household. The mother had invited him saying:

'I do hope you'll be good enough to grace our humble home.'

Even the apoplectic judge who was by her side exclaimed: 'Humble home! Why, it's a palace, dear lady!'

Also present that night were the friend in the straw hat, a

97

decrepit old Knight of Malta, confused and deaf, a priest from the cathedral famous for his treble voice, and the Hilária sisters. The eldest sister, having been present (as nanny to a lady from the Casa da Mina) at the bullfight in Salvaterra during which the Count of Arcos was killed, would endlessly retell picturesque episodes from that afternoon: how the Count looked, clean-shaven and with a scarlet ribbon tied in his pigtail; the sonnet recited by a scrawny poet – a hanger-on at the Casa de Vimioso – just as the Count entered the ring on his prancing horse that was harnessed in Spanish style and wore a saddle cloth bearing the Count's coat of arms embroidered in silver; the terrible tumble a Franciscan friar took from the high barrier and the hilarity of the Court – even the Countess of Povolide was seen clutching her sides in laughter. Then there was King José I, dressed in scarlet velvet embroidered with gold, leaning back in his chair on the dais, fingering his jewel-encrusted snuff box, and behind him, utterly still, stood his physician Dr Lourenço and his confessor; then there was the splendid bullring packed with people from Salvaterra – landowners, beggars, priests, lackeys – and the cry that went up when King José entered: Long live the King! And the people knelt and then the King sat down, eating sweets out of a velvet bag carried by a maid. And then there was the death of the Count, with people fainting, the King bent double, beating with his hand on the parapet, shouting above the hubbub, and the chaplain from Casa dos Arcos who rushed into the ring to administer the last rites. Hilária had been transfixed with fear, she could hear the moans of the oxen, the shrill cries of the women, the hysterical shouting of those who had fainted, then she saw an old man all dressed in black velvet wielding a slender sword and being restrained by various ladies and gentlemen from hurling himself into the ring, bellowing with rage! 'It's the Count's father.' Then she too had fainted in the arms of a priest. When she came to, she found herself outside the bullring. The royal carriage was at the door; the coachmen wore feathers in their hats, the mules had bells on their harnesses and the postilions carried lances. The King was inside, huddled with his confessor in the darkness, deathly pale and taking feverish pinches of snuff; opposite him – strong, broad-shouldered, grave-faced, resting his hands on a tall walking stick – sat the Marquis of Pombal talking in measured, confiding tones, gesticulating with his pince-nez. The postilions cracked their whips and the carriage left at a gallop while the crowd again cried: 'Long live the King!' And the bell at the door of the palace chapel tolled the death knell: an honour bestowed on the Casa dos Arcos by the King.

When, with a final sigh, the eldest of the Hilária sisters concluded her account of those sad events, the games began. Macário could not remember a single game they played that radiant night. He only remembered that he remained by the side of the young blonde woman, whose name was Luísa, and that he was keenly aware of her fine, rosy skin touched by the light, her soft, adorably small hands and her nails more highly polished than Dieppe ivory; he remembered too an odd incident which, from that day forth, provoked in him a great hostility towards the clergy of the cathedral. Macário was sitting at a table next to Luísa. Luísa was facing him, one hand supporting her lovely blonde head and the other lying in her lap. Opposite them sat the priest from the cathedral, with his black biretta, his glasses perched on the end of his sharp nose, the bluish tone of his heavy shaven jowls, and his large, hairy, complicated ears like two open doors on either side of his head. Now, since, at the end of the game, it was necessary to pay one's dues to the Knight of Malta who was sitting beside the priest, Macário had taken a coin out of his pocket and while the Knight, all bent and with one eye twitching, was adding up the sums on the back of a card, Macário continued talking to Luísa and spinning his gold coin on the green baize like a bobbin or a top. It was a new coin that gleamed and glittered as it spun, looking like a ball of golden mist. Luísa was smiling as she watched it spin and spin and it seemed to Macário that all heaven, all purity, all the goodness of flowers and all the chasteness of stars lay in that bright, distracted, spiritual smile, worthy of an archangel, as she watched the spinning of that bright new gold coin. Suddenly, the coin rolled to the edge of the table, fell to one side into Luísa's lap and disappeared, with no clink of metal on wood as it fell to the floor. The priest politely bent down and Macário pushed back his chair in order to look under the table, while Luísa's mother held a candle to help with the search and Luísa jumped up and shook her dress. The gold coin was nowhere to be found.

'How very odd,' said Macário's friend, the one with the straw hat, 'I didn't hear it fall to the floor.'

'Neither did I,' everyone said.

Bent double, the priest was still tenaciously searching and the youngest of the Hilária sisters was mumbling a prayer to St Anthony.

'It must have fallen down a hole,' Luísa's mother was saying.

'It can't just disappear like that,' the priest was muttering.

Meanwhile Macário kept uttering desperate, disinterested cries of:

'Really, what does it matter? It'll turn up tomorrow! Please, I beg you ... Really, Dona Luísa! Please, it's really not worth it.'

Mentally, though, he noted that someone must have taken it and he blamed the priest. The gold coin had doubtless rolled silently towards him, he had placed his great, dirty ecclesiastical shoe on top of it and then adroitly pocketed it, the villain! On their way out, the priest, all wrapped up in his great camel-hair cloak, was saying to Macário as they went down the stairs:

'What do you think of that coin disappearing? A fine how-do-you-do, eh!'

'Do you think so, sir?' said Macário pausing, amazed at the fellow's impudence.

'Of course I do! What do *you* think? A gold coin worth 7,000 *réis*! Or maybe your gold coins grow on trees. I'd be furious!'

Macário was bored by this display of cool astuteness. He gave no reply. The priest added:

'You send someone over here tomorrow. It's the very devil

. . . God forgive me . . . it really is. You can't lose a gold coin just like that. What a game, eh!'

And Macário felt like striking him.

It was at that point that Macário said to me, in a mournful voice:

'Anyway, my friend, to cut a long story short, I decided to marry her.'

'And the gold coin?'

'I thought no more about it. Why should I? I had just decided to marry Luísa!'

2

Macário told me what exactly had brought about that deep and binding resolve. It was a kiss. But I will say nothing about that chaste and simple matter because the only witness was an engraving of the Virgin hanging in a blackwood frame in the dark sitting room that opened onto the stairs. It was a fleeting, superficial, ethereal kiss, but, being a man of correct, even severe character, Macário took it as an obligation to take her as his wife, to give her his word of honour and possession of his life. And thus they were betrothed. For him, the nice coincidence of their facing windows had gained the significance of a destiny, had become the moral end of his life and the guiding light of his work. His story, of course, now takes on the lofty character of sanctity and sadness.

Macário told me a lot about the nature and appearance of Uncle Francisco: his imposing stature, his gold-rimmed spectacles, his greying beard which he grew like a fringe about his jawline, the nervous tic he had in one nostril, the harshness of his voice, his austere, majestic calm, his ancient, authoritarian, tyrannical principles and the telegraphic brevity of his words.

When Macário said to him one morning at breakfast, completely out of the blue: 'I want to get married,' Uncle Francisco, who was spooning sugar into his coffee, remained silent and continued stirring, slowly, majestically, dauntingly. When he had finished slurping his coffee noisily out of the saucer, he removed his napkin from his collar, folded it up, sharpened a toothpick with his knife, put the toothpick in his mouth and left. At the door he stopped and, turning to Macário who was standing by the table, he said simply:

'No.'

'Please, Uncle Francisco!'

'No.'

'But listen, Uncle Francisco.'

'No.'

Macário felt enraged.

'In that case, I'll do it without your permission.'

'I'll throw you out of the house.'

'Don't worry, I'll go.'

'Today.'

'Today.'

Uncle Francisco was just about to close the door when he turned round:

'I say,' he said to Macário who was standing exasperated, apoplectic, clawing at the window pane.

Macário turned round hopefully.

'Give me my snuffbox, will you,' said Uncle Francisco.

He had forgotten his snuffbox, that was all he was worried about.

'Uncle Francisco,' began Macário.

'That's enough. It's the twelfth today. You'll be paid for the whole month. Now go.'

The mores of the time provoked these foolish situations. It was brutal, idiotic. Macário said as much.

That evening Macário found himself in the room of a hostelry in the Praça da Figueira with six coins in his pocket, a trunk full of personal linen, and his love. Nevertheless, he felt quite calm. The future bristled with difficulties, but he had relatives and friends in the business. He had a good reputation; the neatness of his work, his traditional honesty, the name of the family, his business sense, his beautiful italic hand, meant that the doors of every office stood wide open to him. The next day, in cheerful mood, he went to see Faleiro, a former business contact.

'I'd be glad to take you on, my friend,' he said, 'who wouldn't? But if I do, I'll be in bad odour with your uncle whom I've known for twenty years. He told me so categorically. So you see . . . it's a case of force majeure. I'm very sorry, but . . .'

And everyone Macário went to, confident that he had a good relationship with them, said that they were all afraid of getting in bad odour with his uncle whom they had known for twenty years.

And everyone was 'sorry, but . . .'

Macário went to new businessmen, especially foreign ones, who were unfamiliar with his business or his family connections. He hoped to find people who had not known his uncle for twenty years. But to them, Macário was an unknown quantity, as were his dignity and his skill at his work. If they sought references, they found out that he had been sacked on the spot by his uncle because of a blonde girl in a muslin dress. They looked less sympathetically on Macário. Commerce does not much like sentimental book-keepers. So Macário was beginning to feel that he was in a tight corner. Searching, asking, searching again, the time passed, eating away, penny by penny, at his six gold coins.

Macário moved to a cheaper lodging house and continued looking. However, since he had always been of a timid nature, he did not make friends. He found himself alone and helpless; his life stretched before him like a desert.

His money ran out. Macário gradually became part of the ancient tradition of poverty. It has its fateful, established rituals: he began by going to the pawn shop. Then he sold things. A watch, rings, a blue tailcoat, his gold chain, a braided jacket, they were all carried off one by one, wrapped up in a shawl, by a withered, asthmatic old crone.

Meanwhile, he saw Luísa every night, in the dark little living-room that opened onto the landing; a night-light burned on the table. He was happy in that half-darkness, sitting chastely by Luísa's side at one end of an old wicker sofa. He never saw her during the day because now he had to wear second-hand clothes, his boots were worn and he did not want Luísa, so fresh and pretty in her clean chambray, to see his darned and patched poverty. There in that pale, flickering light, he would speak of his growing passion and hide his declining fate. According to Macário, Luísa had a most unusual temperament. Her character was as blonde as her hair, if you consider blonde to be a weak, insipid colour. She spoke little, but smiled constantly, showing her small white teeth and saying 'Of course' to everything. She was simple, compliant, almost indifferent.

She doubtless loved Macário, but only with the kind of love her feeble, watery, vacuous nature was capable of. She was like a skein of flax, you could spin her as you wished. Sometimes, she even grew drowsy during those night-time encounters.

One day, however, Macário found her in a state of great agitation. She was in a hurry, she had her shawl on crooked, and kept looking round all the time at the door.

'Mama knows something,' she said.

And she told him that her mother was suspicious, indeed sullen and resentful, and that she was bound to find out about their wedding plans which they had been making almost conspiratorially.

'Why don't you ask my mother for my hand?'

'I can't. I have no work. Wait a little longer – another month perhaps. I'm in the process of closing a deal now . . . We would starve, Luísa.'

Luísa fell silent. She stood there twisting the end of her shawl, her eyes lowered.

'All right,' she said, 'but promise you won't visit again until I give you a sign from the window.'

Macário burst into tears; his sobs were violent, desperate.

'Shh!' said Luísa. 'Don't make so much noise!'

Macário described to me the night he spent wandering the streets in his light jacket, shivering in the harsh January wind, feverishly pondering his sorrows. He did not sleep and first thing the next morning he burst into Uncle Francisco's room.

'This is all I've got,' he said abruptly, showing him the three coins in his hand. 'I have no clothes. I've sold everything. Before too long, I'll be starving.'

Uncle Francisco, who was shaving, standing at the window with an Indian scarf tied around his head, turned round, put on his glasses and looked at him.

'Your desk is over there. All you have to do,' he said making a resolute gesture, 'is to stay single.'

'Uncle Francisco, listen to me!'

'Single, I said,' repeated Uncle Francisco, sharpening his razor.

'I can't.'

'Then leave this house at once!'

Stunned, Macário left. He returned to his lodgings, lay down on his bed and cried himself to sleep. When he went out that evening he had no idea what to do. He felt drained. He let his feet lead them where they would.

Suddenly, someone from inside a shop shouted to him:

'Hey! Over here!'

It was his friend in the straw hat who opened his arms wide in amazement.

'Good grief, I've been looking for you since this morning.'

He told Macário that he had just got back from the provinces, that he had learned of his plight and had brought him a solution.

'Are you interested?'

'Absolutely.'

A business house wanted an able man, resolute and brave, to go on a difficult, but lucrative mission to Cape Verde.

'Right,' said Macário, 'I'll leave tomorrow.'

He wrote immediately to Luísa, asking her to grant him at least a farewell, one final meeting, one from which the desolate, passionate arms of lovers would find it painful to disentwine. He went to see her. He found her all wrapped up in her shawl, shivering with cold. Macário wept. With her usual blonde, passive sweetness, she said to him:

'You're doing the right thing. You might even make some money.'

The next day Macário left.

He experienced difficult voyages through hostile seas, the monotony of seasickness in a stifling cabin, the harsh colonial sun, the tyrannical brutality of rich landowners, the weight of humiliating burdens, the lacerating pain of absence, journeys into the interior of dark lands and the melancholy of boats that travel through stormy nights, for days on end, along calm rivers redolent of death.

He returned home.

That same evening he saw Luísa, bright, fresh, rested and serene, leaning on the windowsill, fanning herself with the Chinese fan. The next day, as a matter of urgency, he went to ask her mother for her daughter's hand in marriage. Macário had earned a lot of money while he was away and her mother, full of joyful exclamations, opened her large, friendly arms to him. It was decided that he and Luísa would get married in a year's time.

'Why so long?' I asked Macário.

And he explained to me that the money he had earned in Cape Verde would not give him enough capital. It was only enough to set himself up in business, but he had brought back from Cape Verde the beginnings of a great enterprise; he would work like a Trojan for a year and at the end of that he would easily be able to afford to bring up a family.

He worked. He put into that work all the creative force of his passion. He would get up at dawn, eat a hasty breakfast, barely speaking to a soul. In the evening he would visit Luísa. Then he would rush back to his work, like a miser to his coffers. He was well-built, strong, hard, vigorous; he used ideas and muscles with equal energy; he lived in a storm of figures. Sometimes Luísa would come into his shop and the sight of that fugitive bird alighting in his world gave him enough joy, courage, faith and comfort for a whole hard-working month.

Around that time, his friend with the straw hat came to ask Macário if he would stand guarantor for a large sum of money he was borrowing in order to set up an ironmongery business. Macário, who was well in credit, agreed happily. It was the same friend who had provided him with that providential business opportunity in Cape Verde. There were only two months to go before his marriage. Sometimes Macário's face flushed with hope. He set about getting the banns published. One day, however, his friend in the straw hat disappeared with the wife of a corporal. He had barely begun setting up his business. It was a confusing affair. It is impossible to give a clear explanation of the whole painful mess. Macário was the guarantor, that much was certain; he would have to repay the loan. When he found out, he went deathly pale and said simply:

'I'll sell up and pay it off!'

Once he had sold up, he was poor again. But that same day – for this disastrous affair had gained a lot of publicity and public opinion was firmly on his side – the firm of Peres & Co who had first sent him to Cape Verde came to propose a second voyage and further profits.

'Go back to Cape Verde?' Macário exclaimed.

'And make another fortune. You've got the luck of the devil, you have!' said Senhor Eleutério Peres.

When he saw the situation he was in, alone and poor, Macário wept bitterly. Everything was lost, finished, dead; he would patiently have to restart his life, return to the long miseries of Cape Verde, re-experience past despairs, sweat the same sweat again! And Luísa? Macário wrote to her. Then he tore up the letter. He went to her house. There was a light on in the window; he went up to the first floor, but was gripped by grief, by cowardice; he was afraid to tell her about the disaster; he was filled by the terrible fear of another separation, the terror that she would refuse him, deny him, hesitate. Would she want to wait any longer? He did not dare to speak, explain, ask questions; he went slowly back down the stairs. It was dark outside. He wandered through the streets; it was a night of calm, silent moonlight. He hardly noticed where he was walking and then suddenly, from a lighted window, he heard someone playing a Moorish ballad on a recorder. He remembered the first time he had seen Luísa: the bright sunlight, her blue-spotted muslin dress. He was in the street where his uncle had his shop. He continued walking. He stopped to look up at his former home. The window of his old office was closed. From there he had so often watched Luísa and the gentle fluttering of her Chinese fan. One window, on the second floor, was lit; it was his uncle's room. Macário took a closer look; he could see a figure at the window; it was his Uncle Francisco. He felt a sudden nostalgia for his whole simple, solitary, placid past. He remembered his room and the old desk with the silver lock and the miniature of his mother above the bedstead; the dining-room with its old blackwood sideboard and the great water jug with a handle made in the shape of an angry serpent. Impelled by some instinct, he decided to knock at the door. He knocked again. He heard the window open and his uncle's voice ask:

'Who is it?'

'It's me, Uncle Francisco, it's me. I've come to say goodbye.'

The window closed and shortly afterwards the door opened with a great clanking of locks. Uncle Francisco was carrying an oil lamp in his hand. Macário thought he looked thinner, older. He kissed his hand.

'Come up,' said his uncle.

Macário followed him in silence, keeping close to the bannister.

When they reached his room, Uncle Francisco placed the lamp on a broad table and stood there, his hands in his pockets, waiting.

Macário smoothed his beard and said nothing.

'Well, what do you want?' his uncle asked loudly.

'I came to say goodbye. I'm going back to Cape Verde.'

'Then I hope you have a good journey.'

And his Uncle Francisco turned his back on him and stood drumming his fingers on the window.

Macário froze, then took a few indignant steps about the room and made to leave.

'Where are you going, you idiot?' his uncle shouted.

'I'm leaving.'

'Sit down!' his uncle said and continued talking, at the same time striding about the room:

'Your friend is a good-for-nothing! An ironmonger's of all things! You're a good man. Stupid, but a good man. Sit down, sit down! Your friend is a good-for-nothing! You're a good man! You went to Cape Verde! I know that! You paid every-thing back. Of course. I know that too. Tomorrow, I want you to return to your desk downstairs. I've ordered a new seat for your chair. On the bill I want you to write: Macário & Nephew. And get married. Get married if that's what you want to do. Draw some money out too. You need some new linen and some furniture. And put it on my account. Your bed is made up next door.'

Macário wanted to embrace him, he was stunned, he had tears in his eyes, he was beaming broadly.

'Fine, fine; I'll be off then!'

Macário was about to leave.

'You young fool, why would you want to leave your own home?'

He went over to a small cupboard and produced some jelly, a saucer of jam, an old bottle of port and some biscuits.

'Eat.'

He sat next to Macário, again called him a fool, and one tear ran down his wrinkled skin.

The marriage was to take place in a month's time. Luísa started putting together her trousseau.

Macário was overwhelmed with love and happiness.

His life seemed to him full, complete, happy. He spent most of his time at his fiancée's house and one day he accompanied her to the shops. He wanted to buy her a little present. Her mother had stayed behind at the dressmaker's, on the first floor of a building in Rua do Ouro, and Macário and Luísa had gone happily down the stairs to a goldsmith's below in the same building.

It was a bright winter's day, fine and cold, with a vast, electric-blue sky, deep, luminous, consoling.

'What a lovely day,' Macário said.

With his fiancée on his arm, he walked a little way along the pavement.

'It is,' she said, 'but people might notice us out alone like this . . .'

'Come on, it's so nice . . .'

'No.'

And Luísa dragged him gently towards the jeweller's. There was only one assistant, a swarthy chap with a lot of hair.

Macário said to him:

'I'd like to see some rings.'

'With stones,' said Luísa, 'the prettiest you have.'

'Yes, with stones,' said Macário. 'Amethysts, garnets. The best you've got.'

Meanwhile, Luísa was examining the displays in their blue velvet-lined cases glittering with heavy jewel-encrusted bracelets, chains, cameo necklaces, signet rings, slender wedding rings as fragile as love and a whole glinting world of heavy goldwork.

'Look, Luísa,' said Macário.

At the far end of the counter, on top of the glass display cabinet, the assistant had laid out a shimmering spread of golden rings, rings set with stones, engraved and enamelled, and Luísa, picking them up and putting them down again with the tips of her fingers went through all of them saying:

'Too ugly. Too heavy. Too big.'

'Look at this one,' said Macário.

It was a ring made out of little pearls.

'Oh, how pretty,' she said. 'Really lovely!'

'See if it fits you,' said Macário.

And taking her hand, he put the ring slowly, tenderly on her finger, and she laughed, showing her small white teeth like enamel.

'What a shame,' said Macário, 'it's much too big!'

'We can make it smaller if you want. Just give us the measurement. We can have it ready for you tomorrow.'

'That's a good idea,' said Macário, 'yes, indeed. It really is very pretty, isn't it? The pearls are so well-matched in size, and so bright. Very pretty. And what about those earrings?' he added, moving to the end of the counter to another display cabinet. 'Those ones shaped like a shell.'

'They cost ten *moedas*,' said the assistant.

And meanwhile Luísa continued examining the rings, trying them on all her fingers, rummaging through that delicate, glittering, precious display.

Suddenly the assistant turned very pale and looked hard at Luísa, passing a hand slowly over his face.

'Right,' said Macário, going over to him, 'so you'll have the ring ready for us tomorrow. What time?'

111

The assistant did not reply and began to look hard at Macário.

'What time?'

'At midday.'

'Fine,' said Macário. 'We'll see you tomorrow then.'

They were just about to leave. Luísa was wearing a blue woollen dress that dragged a little along the ground, giving a melodious sway to her walk, and her small hands were hidden inside a white muff.

'Excuse me,' the assistant said suddenly.

Macário turned round.

'You haven't paid.'

Macário looked at him gravely.

'Of course I haven't. I'll pay you when I come to pick up the ring tomorrow.'

'I'm sorry,' said the assistant, 'but you haven't paid for the other ring.'

'What other ring?' said Macário, surprised, going over to the counter.

'That lady knows what I mean,' said the assistant.

Macário slowly took out his wallet.

'I'm sorry, if it's some unsettled bill . . .'

The assistant came out from behind the counter and with a resolute look on his face said:

'No, it's not an old bill, sir, it's a new one. It's for a ring with two diamonds in it which that lady has taken.'

'Me!' said Luísa in a low voice, her face scarlet.

'What? What do you mean?'

Pale-faced, his teeth clenched, rigid with tension, Macário stared furiously at the assistant.

The assistant said:

'That lady took a ring from the counter.' Macário didn't move; he was still staring into the assistant's face. 'A ring with two diamonds. I saw her myself.' The assistant was so upset he was stammering, horribly embarrassed. 'I don't know who the lady is, but she definitely took the ring.'

Macário seized him by the arm and turned to Luísa, barely

able to speak. His face ashen, beads of sweat standing out on his forehead, he said at last:

'Luísa, say something,' but his voice faltered.

'I . . .,' she began. She was trembling, terrified, transfixed, shaken.

She had dropped her muff on the floor.

Macário went over to her, grabbed her wrist and looked at her. His look was so determined, so imperious, that she hastily, fearfully put her hand into her pocket and showed him the ring.

'Don't hurt me,' she said, cringing.

Macário stood there, abstracted, his lips blanched, his arms hanging inert at his sides. Then, giving a tug at his jacket, he recovered himself and said to the assistant:

'You're quite right. A mistake, of course. The lady forgot. The ring, yes, of course . . . if you wouldn't mind. Give it to me, dear. This gentleman will wrap it up for you. How much is it?'

He opened his wallet and paid.

Then he picked up the muff, gently brushed it off, dabbed at his lips with a handkerchief, gave his arm to Luísa, and saying to the assistant 'I'm so sorry, so very sorry', he led her out of the shop, inert, passive, cowed and terrified.

They walked a little way down the street. Long rays of sun lit up the happy scene: carriages passed, rolling by to the crack of a whip; people passed, smiling and talking; streetsellers cheerily cried their wares; a horseman in suede breeches was making his horse, all adorned with rosettes, prance down the street; the street was crowded, noisy, alive, happy and sunny.

Macário was walking along mechanically as if in a dream. He stopped on a corner. Luísa had her arm linked in his. He saw her hand hanging there, waxen, the veins pale blue, her adorable, slender fingers: it was her right hand and that hand belonged to his fiancée. Out of pure habit he read a poster advertising for that night: *Palafox of Zaragoza*.

Suddenly, he let go of Luísa's arm and said to her in a low voice:

'Go away.'

113

'Listen,' she said, leaning towards him.

'Go away.' And his voice sounded hoarse and terrible. 'Go or I'll call the police. I'll have you sent to prison. Just go away.'

'Please, for the love of God, listen,' she said.

'Go away,' he repeated and made a gesture with his clenched fist.

'Dear God, please don't hit me,' she said, overcome.

'Just go away, people might notice. Don't cry. People will see. Go.'

And moving closer to her he said:

'You're a thief.'

Turning his back on her, he walked slowly away, trailing his walking stick along the ground.

When he had walked some distance, he turned round; he could still see her blue dress among the crowds.

He left for the provinces that evening and never heard another word about that blonde young woman.

THE HANGED MAN

1

In the year of 1474, a year bountiful in divine mercies for all of Christendom, when King Henry IV still reigned in Castile, a gentleman came to live in the town of Segovia where he had inherited a house and some land. His name was Don Ruy de Cárdenas, a young man of pure lineage and handsome appearance.

The house had been left to him by his uncle, an archdeacon and a teacher of canon law, and was built in the silent shadow of the Church of Our Lady of the Pillar. Opposite, beyond the courtyard, where water bubbled from the three spouts of an ancient fountain, there stood a dark palace with barred windows which belonged to Don Alonso de Lara, an extremely wealthy nobleman of sombre mien who, in the autumn of his years when his hair was already threaded with silver, had married a young girl famed in all Castile for her white skin, her hair the colour of bright sunlight and her neck as long and slender as a heron's. It so happened that Our Lady of the Pillar had been Don Ruy's patroness since birth and he had remained a devoted and loyal servant ever since, despite being a cheerful, hotblooded young man who took pleasure in weaponry, hunting, courtly gatherings, as well as the occasional rowdy night in a tavern playing dice and downing pitchers of wine. Out of love and in view of the fact that his holy patroness was now his close neighbour, he had, ever since his arrival in Segovia, acquired the pious habit of visiting Her each morning at prime to say three Hail Marys and to ask for Her blessing and Her grace.

Even after a vigorous ride over hill and dale with his greyhounds or his falcon, he would always be back as darkness fell in time for vespers, in order to murmur one more sweet Hail Mary.

And every Sunday he would buy a bunch of jonquils or

carnations or roses from a Moorish girl who sold flowers in the courtyard and these he would strew before the altar of Our Lady with gallant tenderness and care.

Another regular Sunday visitor to this venerated church was Doña Leonor, Señor de Lara's extraordinarily beautiful and much talked-of wife who would arrive accompanied by a sullen maid with eyes rounder and keener than a screech owl's, and flanked by two powerfully-built lackeys who guarded her like two towers. Don Alonso was so jealous that he permitted this fleeting visit only because his confessor had ordered him to do so and out of fear of offending his neighbour, Our Lady of the Pillar, but all the time his wife was away he would peer anxiously out from behind the shutters, watching every move she made and gauging just how long she spent in the church. Doña Leonor spent each slow day of each slow week shut up behind the barred windows of the black granite palace with, as her sole place of recreation and freedom, even in the heat of summer, a small, gloomy garden surrounded by walls so high that only the tip of a sad cypress tree could occasionally be glimpsed above them. However, that brief visit to Our Lady of the Pillar was enough for Don Ruy to fall hopelessly in love with her on the May morning when he first saw her kneeling before the altar, caught in a beam of light, her golden hair like a halo about her head, her long lashes lowered as she read her Book of Hours, her rosary slipping through her slender fingers, indeed, everything about her was slender, soft and white, the whiteness of a lily blooming in the shadows, even whiter when set amongst the black laces and satins that fell in stiff folds about her graceful figure, brushing the chapel flagstones which were, in fact, ancient tombstones. When, after a moment of delicious, spellbound enchantment, he knelt down, he was not really kneeling to the Virgin of the Pillar, his holy patroness, but to that mortal apparition whose name he did not even know, but for whom he would give up both name and life, were she willing to surrender herself for such an uncertain prize. With indecent haste, he managed to stammer out the three Hail Marys with which he greeted Our Lady each morning, then he snatched up his hat, walked briskly down the echoing nave and waited for Doña Leonor in the doorway amongst the starving beggars sitting in the sun picking lice off themselves. After a period of time during which Don Ruy felt his heart beating with unaccustomed anxiety and fear, Doña Leonor finally passed by, pausing only to moisten her fingers in the marble stoup of holy water; however, she did not so much as glance up at him, either timidly or by chance. With her round-eyed maid glued to her side, flanked by the two towering lackeys, she slowly crossed the courtyard, stone by stone, doubtless savouring, like a prisoner, the open air and the sunlight filling it. And it was with horror that Don Ruy watched her walk along the sombre arcade, past the great pillars upon which the palace was built, and disappear through a narrow door reinforced with iron studs. So she was the famous Doña Leonor, the lovely and noble Señora de Lara.

Thus began seven long days which he spent sitting at his window, watching that black, iron-studded door as if it were the gate to Paradise that might suddenly swing open to reveal an angel bearing glad tidings. At last, Sunday came round again, and as he was walking across the courtyard at prime when the bells were ringing, carrying a bunch of yellow carnations for his holy patroness, Doña Leonor crossed his path as she emerged from amongst the pillars of the dark arcade, sweet, white and pensive, like the moon appearing from among clouds. In the pleasurable tumult that made his chest rise and fall like the sea and his soul rush forth from him in one all-devouring gaze, he almost dropped the carnations. She returned his gaze, but her eyes were calm, serene, betraying not a glimmer of curiosity, barely conscious of meeting someone else's eyes, eyes inflamed and darkened by desire. The young gentleman did not go into the church, out of a pious fear that he would be unable to give his holy patroness the attention She deserved, the attention stolen from him by that purely human creature who was, nonetheless, already the divine mistress of his heart.

He waited impatiently at the door, along with the beggars, the carnations wilting in his hot, trembling hands, thinking only how long she was lingering over her rosary. Even as

Doña Leonor was walking down the nave, he could already sense in his soul the sweet rustle of her stiff silks as they dragged across the flagstones. The pale lady passed by and bestowed upon him the same distracted gaze, inattentive and calm, that she bestowed upon the beggars in the courtyard, either because she could not understand why the young man standing there should suddenly turn so pale or because she could not as yet distinguish him from any of the other indifferent shapes and objects.

Don Ruy gave a deep sigh and fled. Then, once back in his room, he devoutly placed before the image of the Virgin the flowers he had failed to place upon Her altar in the church. His whole life became a long lament at the coldness and inhumanity of that woman, unique among all women, who had captured his heart and made serious what before had been light and fickle. Full of hope, though he knew beforehand that he would be disappointed, he began to patrol the high garden walls or, wrapped in a cape, leaning at a corner, he would spend long hours contemplating the bars on the windows, thick and black as prison bars. Not a single beam of optimistic light emerged from between the bars, nor were there any chinks in the walls. The whole palace was like a tomb built for a woman devoid of feeling and beyond the cold stones lay an equally cold heart. He poured his feelings onto parchment in two mournful ballads which he toiled over during sleepless nights, but they did nothing to relieve him. He knelt before the altar of Our Lady of the Pillar, on the same stones on which he had seen Doña Leonor kneel, and he remained there, unable to pray, immersed in bittersweet thoughts, waiting for his heart to find calm and consolation under the influence of She who consoles and calms everything. However, he always rose to his feet feeling even more wretched than before, conscious only of how cold and hard were the stones on which he had knelt. Indeed, the whole world seemed hard and cold.

He encountered Doña Leonor on subsequent bright Sunday mornings, but her eyes always appeared indifferent, distracted or, if they did meet his, so innocent and so empty of emotion, that Don Ruy would have preferred it had they shown disgust or glinted with rage or looked proudly and disdainfully away from him. Doña Leonor clearly recognised him now, but only insofar as she also recognised the Moorish flowergirl squatting by her basket near the fountain or the poor people who lay in the sun by the main door delousing themselves. Now Don Ruy could not even think of her as inhuman and cold. She was merely regally remote, like a star that turns and glitters in the heavens, unaware that below, in a world she cannot perceive, eyes she knows nothing of gaze up at her, adore her and surrender to her the government of their fortunes and their happiness.

Then Don Ruy thought: 'She doesn't want me, there's nothing I can do about it; it was simply a dream that died. May Our Lady keep us both in Her grace.'

Being a most discreet gentleman, once he had recognised her unshakeable indifference towards him, he no longer sought her out, he no longer gazed up at the bars on her windows, he would not even go into the church now if, from the doorway, he happened to see her kneeling there, her graceful, golden head bent over her Book of Hours.

2

The old serving woman, the one with eyes as round and hard as a screech owl's, lost no time in telling Señor de Lara that a bold young man of elegant appearance, the new owner of the house that had once belonged to the archdeacon, was always to be found pacing the courtyard or standing in front of the church itself in order to catch the eye of Señora Doña Leonor. The jealous nobleman was already bitterly aware of this fact, since, as he watched like a hawk from his window as the graceful lady made her way to church, he had observed the young gallant pacing up and down, seen the darting looks he gave Doña Leonor and had plucked furiously at his beard. Indeed, ever since then, he had poured all his energies into hating Don Ruy, the canon's impudent nephew, who had dared to make the exalted Señora de Lara the focus of his base desires. He ordered a servant to watch Don Ruy continually and thus knew all his comings and goings, the names of his hunting and drinking companions, even the name of his tailor and of the man who polished his sword, indeed, he knew what Don Ruy did at every waking moment. He watched over Doña Leonor even more anxiously, he observed her every movement, every fleeting mood, her silences, her conversations with the maids, her daydreams over her embroidery, the way she gazed out at the trees in the garden, and how she behaved and whether she was flushed or pale when she returned from church. But Doña Leonor seemed so unalterably calm, so serene of heart, that not even the most imaginatively jealous husband eager to find fault could discover a single stain on that pure white snow. Don Alonso's rancour towards the archdeacon's nephew redoubled in strength, simply because Don Ruy had dared to desire Doña Leonor's purity, her hair the colour of bright sunlight and her neck long and slender as a heron's, all of which were Don Alonso's alone, for him alone to glory in. It was always that same bitter thought that kept going round and round in his head when he walked the gloomy gallery of the echoing, vaulted palace in his sheepskin coat edged with fur, the point of his greying beard sticking out before him, his mane of curly hair bristling behind him, his fists clenched.

'He impugned her virtue and impugned my honour. He is doubly guilty and therefore deserves to die a double death.'

But his fury became mingled with terror when he learned that Don Ruy no longer waited in the courtyard for Doña Leonor to pass, that he had abandoned his amorous patrolling of the palace walls and never went into the church when she prayed there on Sundays; indeed, so indifferent had Don Ruy become to her that one morning, when he was in the arcade and must have heard the creak of the door through which the lady would appear, he had remained with his back turned to her, unmoved, laughing with a plump gentleman who was reading to him from a parchment. Such artfully affected indifference doubtless served only to hide some truly evil intention (or so thought Don Alonso). What was that skilful deceiver plotting? The grotesque old man grew ever more deranged, his jealousy, his rancour, his vigilance more intense. In Doña Leonor's serenity he saw only cunning and pretence and immediately forbade her visits to Our Lady of the Pillar.

On those mornings, he himself would run to the church to say the rosary and to offer Doña Leonor's apologies, 'She can't come' (he would murmur as he bent before the altar) 'for reasons you yourself know, Most Holy Virgin.' He carefully checked and reinforced all the locks on the gates to his palace.

At night, he unleashed two mastiffs to roam the shadows of the walled gardens.

He kept an unsheathed sword at the head of the vast bed, by the table on which stood a lamp, a reliquary and a glass of warm wine spiced with an invigorating mix of cinnamon and cloves. However, despite these security measures, he barely slept and was constantly starting up from the soft pillows, grasping Doña Leonor round the throat with his desperate, brutish hands and hissing in her ear in anxious tones: 'Tell me that you love only me!' Then, at dawn, he would return like a hawk to his perch to keep watch on Don Ruy's windows. Not that he ever saw him now, either at the door of the church when it was the hour for Mass, or riding in from the country as the Hail Mary was rung.

Seeing that Don Ruy had disappeared from all his accustomed haunts, Don Alonso became even more convinced that the former had won Doña Leonor's heart.

Then one night, after much pacing up and down on the stone slabs of the gallery, with his thoughts mired in distrust and hatred, he called his steward and ordered that trunks be packed and horses prepared. Early the next morning he would leave with Doña Leonor for his property in Cabril, two leagues from Segovia. They did not depart at dawn, however, like a miser fleeing to find some distant place wherein to hide his treasure, instead the move was carried out very slowly and ostentatiously: the litter stood for hours in the arcade, the curtains wide open, while a stable boy walked up and down the courtyard leading Don Alonso's white mule decked out in Moorish style; outside the garden gate the mules were hitched to iron rings on the wall where they stood laden with trunks beneath the hot sun and the flies, filling the alleyway with a tinkling of bells. Thus Don Ruy learned of Señor de Lara's departure, as indeed did the whole of Segovia.

Their departure was a source of great contentment to Doña Leonor who loved Cabril with its lush orchards and gardens onto which the windows of her bright apartments opened, with no bars between; there at least she had plenty of fresh air, sunshine, flowerbeds to water, an aviary, and the paths lined with laurel and yew were so long that just to be able to walk up and down them felt akin to freedom. She hoped, too, that a spell in the country might chase away the cares that had lately made her lord and husband so sullen and taciturn. Her hopes remained unfulfilled; even after a week away, a cloud still hung over Don Alonso, for, of course, no amount of shady trees, murmuring waters or perfumes wafting in on the air from the rosebeds could quieten such deep and bitter turmoil. Just as he had in his palace in Segovia, he would walk restlessly up and down the vaulted, echoing gallery, hunched inside his heavy sheepskin coat, the point of his grey beard sticking out before him, his mane of curly hair bristling behind him, a silent sneer on his lips as if in anticipation of the bitter after-taste of evil deeds as yet unperpetrated. His only interest in life became the servant who galloped back and forth between Segovia and Cabril; he sometimes waited for him on the edge of the village, by the stone cross, anxious to hear the man's news as soon as he dismounted, breathless, from his horse.

One night when Doña Leonor was in her room praying with the maids by the light of a wax taper, Señor de Lara came slowly in, bearing in his hand a sheet of parchment and a quill pen dipped in his own bone inkwell. With a lofty gesture he dismissed the maids who were all as afraid of him as if he were a wolf. Then, drawing a stool up to the table and turning to Doña Leonor with a face that was a picture of tranquillity and affability, as if he had come to see her about some normal, straightforward matter, he said:

'Lady, I would like you to write a most urgent letter for me.'

So trained was she in submission that, unconcerned and incurious, pausing only to place on the bedstead the rosary she had been praying over, she sat down on the stool, picked up the quill in her slender fingers, and with great application, so that her writing should be neat and clear, she wrote the first short line that Señor de Lara dictated, which was: 'My lord,' but when he dictated the next line, which was much longer and spoken in the bitterest of tones, Doña Leonor threw down the quill as if it had burned her and jumped up from the table in great distress, crying:

'Sir, why do you want me to write such falsehoods?'

In an access of rage, Señor de Lara pulled from his belt a dagger which he held to her face, and he snarled:

'If you don't write what I tell you to write and what I want you to write, by God, I'll pierce your heart.'

Turning whiter than the wax taper that lit them both, her skin prickling at the sight of that glinting steel blade, a submissive tremor ran through her and she murmured:

'Mother of God, please don't hurt me! Don't vex yourself so, sir, I want only to serve and obey you. Tell me what I must write and I will write it.'

Leaning his clenched fists on the edge of the table where he had laid down the dagger, and crushing the frail, unhappy woman with his harsh, penetrating gaze, Señor de Lara dictated or, rather, spat out, hoarsely, violently, phrase by phrase, a letter which said, once it was written out in her hesitant, tremulous hand:

My lord,

Either you have failed to understand or else you repay me most cruelly for the love I feel for you, a love I could never show to you clearly when in Segovia. Now I am here in Cabril burning to see you, and if your desire is equal to mine, it can easily be satisfied, for my husband is away visiting another property of his and the house at Cabril is open and easy of access. Come tonight, enter by the garden gate, along the narrow path, by the pool, up to the terrace.

There you will see a ladder leaning against one of the windows, the window to my room where you will find a sweet welcome from one who anxiously awaits you . . .

'Now, lady, sign your name, that's the most important part.'

Doña Leonor slowly wrote her name, blushing as furiously as if she were being made to undress before a crowd of people.

'And now,' ordered her husband in a quieter voice, through clenched teeth, 'address it to Don Ruy de Cárdenas!'

She did not dare look up, surprised by that unfamiliar name.

'Go on! Don Ruy de Cárdenas!' he cried, his face sombre.

And she addressed the false letter to Don Ruy de Cárdenas.

Don Alonso thrust the parchment under his belt, next to the dagger he had replaced in its sheath, and left in silence, his beard preceding him, his steps sounding muffled on the flagstones in the corridor.

Filled by a sense of infinite horror, she remained seated on the stool, her hands lying weary and limp in her lap, her gaze lost in the darkness of the silent night. Death seemed less daunting to her than this dark adventure in which she felt herself caught up, trapped. Who was Don Ruy de Cárdenas, whose name she had never even heard before, who had never so much as brushed her life, so tranquil, so sparsely populated with memories and men? And yet he doubtless knew her, had met her, had at least followed her with his eyes, and so to him, it would seem a natural and inevitable thing to receive a letter of such passion and such promise.

Would a man, doubtless a well-born young man, a nobleman even, thus push his way brusquely into her destiny, led by her husband's hand? So intimately – though quite without her knowledge – was that man bound up in her life that, at night, the garden gate was to be left open for him and a ladder placed against her window for him to climb. And it was her husband who would secretly fling wide the door, who would secretly place the ladder at her window. But why?

Then, in a flash, Doña Leonor understood the truth, the shameful truth. It drew from her a fearful, barely stifled cry. It was a trap. Señor de Lara wanted to lure Don Ruy to Cabril with a magnificent promise, in order to overpower him and doubtless kill him when he was alone and defenceless. And she, her love and her body were the glittering prizes he was dangling before the unfortunate young man's eager eyes. Thus did her husband use her beauty and her bed, as a golden net into which that foolish prey might fall. What greater insult could there be? But how imprudent too! This Don Ruy de Cárdenas might well distrust the offer, reject that openly amorous invitation and then, laughing and triumphant, ride through Segovia brandishing that letter in which the wife of Don Alonso de Lara offered up to him both her body and her bed. But no, the unfortunate man would ride to Cabril and there die a wretched death in the black silence of the night, with no priest, no sacraments, his soul steeped in the sin of love. And die he must, for Señor de Lara would never permit a man who had received such a letter to live. Thus, that young man would die for love of her, for a love which, though it never afforded him a moment's pleasure, would bring him instant death. It seemed to her that love could be the only possible reason; for the kind of hatred Don Alonso de Lara felt, a hatred that bred disloyalty and villainy, could only be born of a jealousy so intense that it overshadowed any sense of duty he felt as a gentleman and a Christian. Doubtless he had observed glances, gestures, intentions on the part of that ill-advised though much-enamoured Don Ruy.

But how? When? She vaguely remembered a young man who had crossed her path one Sunday in the courtyard, who had waited for her at the door of the church with a bunch of carnations in his hands. Was that him? He had been of noble appearance, very pale with large, dark, passionate eyes. She had simply passed by without giving him a thought. The carnations that he held in his hands were red and yellow. Who were they for? If only she could warn him, before dawn broke.

How could she, though, when there was not a single servant or maid in Cabril whom she could trust? Yet how could she allow a brutal, treacherous sword to pierce that heart, a heart so full of love for her, beating only for her, desiring only her!

She imagined Don Ruy's ardent, reckless ride from Segovia to Cabril, with the promise of the enchanted garden standing open, of the ladder leaning against the window, under the silence and protection of night! Would Señor de Lara really order a ladder to be leant against the window? Of course he would, the more easily to kill the poor, sweet, innocent boy when he climbed up, unsteady on the frail rungs, his hands encumbered, his sword asleep in its sheath. Thus, the next night, opposite her bed, her window would stand open and a ladder would be leaning against that window, for a man to climb. Crouched in ambush in the shadows of the room, her husband would be waiting to kill that man.

But what if Señor de Lara chose to lurk outside the garden walls and brutally attack Don Ruy de Cárdenas as he walked along one of the paths and what if, in the ensuing struggle, either because he was less skilled or less strong, he were to fall to the ground dead, without the other man knowing whom he had killed? She would be there in her room, all unsuspecting, with all the doors open and a ladder at her window, and that man would climb the ladder in the soft shadow of the warm night, and the husband who should be there to defend her would be lying dead on a path somewhere. Mother of God, what would she do then? She would, of course, proudly repel the bold youth. He would be shocked and angry to see his desire frustrated. 'But it was you who called me here, lady!' He would be carrying her letter next to his heart, a letter signed by her and written in her hand. How could she explain to him about the ambush and the trap that had been set for him? It would be such a long story to tell in the silence and solitude of the night, while he looked at her pleadingly, piercingly, with those dark, shining eyes . . . Woe to her if Señor de Lara were to die and leave her alone and defenceless in that vast, open house; but woe too if that young man, whom she had invited there and who loved her and who, out of love, would come riding ecstatically to be at her side, were to find death in the place where he thought to find hope, were to find instead the place of his sin, and were to die in sin and thus tumble into eternal despair. If he was the same man she remembered, about twenty-five years old, pale and very elegant, wearing a purple velvet jacket and holding a bunch of carnations in his hand as he stood at the door of the church in Segovia.

Tears welled up in Doña Leonor's weary eyes and, falling to her knees and lifting up her soul to the heavens where the moon was just rising, she murmured in a voice full of infinite sorrow and faith:

'Oh, Holy Virgin of the Pillar, dear Lady, watch over us both, watch over us all!'

129

3

In the silence of the noonday heat, Don Ruy entered the cool courtyard of his house and, as he did so, a country lad sitting on a stone bench in the shadows leapt to his feet, drew forth a letter from inside his shepherd's bag and handed it to him muttering:

'Sir, read this quickly for I have to return at once to Cabril to the person who sent me.'

Don Ruy unfolded the parchment letter, read it and then, overcome by shock, clutched it to his breast as if he would bury it in his heart.

The lad said anxiously:

'Make haste, sir, make haste! There's no need for a reply. I just need some sign that you have received the message.'

Still terribly pale, Don Ruy pulled off one of his silk embroidered gloves which the boy rolled up and stuffed inside his bag; then he ran off on the tips of his light sandals. With a wave, Don Ruy called him back:

'Tell me, which road are you taking to Cabril?'

'The shortest route, but one that is only for the brave of heart: the road that crosses Hangman's Hill.'

'Thanks.'

Don Ruy raced up the stone steps and, without even taking off his hat, stood in his room by the shuttered windows and re-read that divine piece of parchment in which Doña Leonor invited him to her room that night, to possess her entirely. He was not surprised by this offer, even after such a show of constant, implacable indifference. Rather he saw in it a love which, because it was so strong, was also most astute, a love which, confronted by obstacles and dangers, patiently waits and silently prepares for its hour of contentment, and is better and even more delicious for being so well prepared. So she had always loved him, then, from that first, blessed morning when their eyes had met in the doorway of the church. And while he had been circling those garden walls, cursing the coldness that seemed to him colder than the stone walls themselves, she had already given him her soul and constantly, with loving sagacity, had repressed the quietest sigh, silenced all distrust, in preparation for the radiant night when she would also give him her body.

Her determination, her extraordinary ingenuity in these matters of love, made her seem even more beautiful, even more desirable.

With what impatience then did he gaze at the sun which, that evening, seemed reluctant to sink behind the hills. He lingered, restless, in his room, with the shutters closed so that he might more easily ponder his happiness and lovingly prepare everything for his triumphal journey: fine clothes, fine lace, a black velvet jacket and various essential oils. Twice he went down to the stables to check that his horse was well shod and well rested. Several times he tested the blade of the sword he would wear at his waist by flexing it on the ground. But his greatest concern was the road he would take to Cabril, even though he knew it well, as he did the village huddled about the Franciscan monastery and the old Roman bridge with its Calvary, and the narrow path that led to the property owned by Señor de Lara. He had ridden there that winter in order to go hunting in the mountains with two friends from Astorga, and he had seen the tower of the Lara house then and thought: 'There is the tower of my ungrateful love!' How wrong he had been. There was a moon that night and he would leave Segovia silently through the San Mauros Gate. A short gallop would take him as far as Hangman's Hill. He was also familiar with that place of sadness and horror, with its four stone pillars where criminals were hanged and their bodies left to sway in the wind, to be dried by the sun, until the rope rotted and the bleached skeletons fell to the ground to be picked clean by the crows. Behind the hill lay the Lake of Ladies. The last time he had visited the hill was on St Matthew's Day when the mayor and certain charitable brotherhoods had gone there in procession to give sacred burial to the skeletons that had fallen to the black earth. From there the road ran smooth and straight all the way to Cabril.

Thus, while evening fell, Don Ruy meditated upon his happy journey. Then, when it had grown dark and the bats had begun to fly about the church towers, and in the corners of the courtyard candles had been lit for the dead, the brave young man was gripped by a strange fear, a fear of this imminent happiness which seemed to him somehow supernatural. Was it true that in a short time, even before the holy candles lit before the retables had burned out, that divinely beautiful woman, famous in all Castile and inaccessible as a star, would be his, all his, in the silence and safety of her boudoir? And what had he done to deserve such great good fortune? He had paced the flagstones of a courtyard, he had waited in the doorway of a church, trying to catch her eye, but her gaze never raised itself to his, either indifferently or by chance. Then, quite without pain, he had abandoned his hopes and suddenly, that distracted gaze was urgently seeking his, those folded arms were opened to him, long and bare, and that woman was crying out to him body and soul: 'Oh imprudent one, you did not understand me. Come! She who once discouraged you is now yours!' Had there ever been such good fortune, such lofty, rare good fortune, behind which, according to human laws, misfortune must already be lurking? That was the truth of the matter, for what greater misfortune could there be than to know that when dawn broke, he would have to leave behind him that great good fortune, those wondrous arms, and return to Segovia, while his Leonor, the sublime love of his life, so unexpectedly and briefly possessed, would immediately revert to another master!

What did it matter! Let jealousy and sorrow follow afterwards! That splendid night was his alone, the whole world was but vain appearance and the one reality was that dimly lit bedroom in Cabril where she awaited him, her hair loose about her shoulders! He went impatiently down the stairs and leapt onto his horse. Then, out of prudence, he crossed the courtyard very slowly, his hat well back on his head, as if he were just off on a short ride to enjoy the cool of the night

132

outside the city walls. He met no one until he reached the San Mauros Gate. There, a beggar crouched in the darkness of the archway, playing a monotonous tune on the accordion, wailed out a plea to the Virgin and all the Saints to keep that gentle knight in her sweet and holy protection. Don Ruy stopped to give him some alms and suddenly remembered that he had omitted to go to church that evening at vespers, to pray and ask for the blessing of his divine patroness. He jumped down from his horse, for right by the old archway was a flickering lamp illuminating a small shrine. It contained the image of the Virgin with her breast pierced by seven swords. Don Ruy knelt down, placed his hat on the ground and, with his hands raised in prayer, he earnestly said a Hail Mary. A yellow halo of light surrounded the face of Our Lady, whose red lips smiled as if indifferent to the pain from the seven blades that pierced her or as if they were instead a source of ineffable pleasure. While he was praying, the bell began to toll the death knell in the nearby monastery of Santo Domingo. In the black shadows beneath the archway, the accordion music suddenly stopped and the beggar murmured: 'One of the friars is dying.' Don Ruy said a Hail Mary for the dying friar. The Virgin of the seven swords was still smiling sweetly; the death knell was not, therefore, a bad omen, and with renewed heart, Don Ruy remounted and set off.

Beyond the San Mauros Gate, beyond a few hovels inhabited by potters, the road ran, narrow and black, between tall agaves. Behind the hills, at the edge of the dark plain, you could see the first languid, yellow rays of the full moon that was as yet still hidden. Don Ruy trotted on, afraid that he might reach Cabril too early, before the servants had finished their evening's work and said their prayers. Why had Doña Leonor not specified a time in a letter that had otherwise been so clear and so well thought out? His imagination kept racing ahead: he imagined how he would burst into the garden at Cabril, leap lightly up the promised ladder . . . Then he galloped eagerly on, in a wild ride that sent stones flying up from the rough road. He reined in his panting horse. He was early, still too early! He would then resume his slow pace, feeling his heart beating in his breast like a caged bird beating against the bars.

At last he reached the stone cross where the road split in two, the two roads closer than the prongs of a fork, both cutting across through the pinewoods. Doffing his hat before the image of the crucifixion he found there, Don Ruy experienced a moment of anxiety, for he could not remember which path led to Hangman's Hill. He was just setting off down the more overgrown path when, dancing in the darkness, a light appeared amongst the silent pine trees. It was a ragged old woman with long, dishevelled hair, bent over a stick and carrying a candle.

'Where does this road lead?' shouted Don Ruy.

The old woman held the candle higher to get a better look at the gentleman.

'To Xarama.'

And with that, both the light and the old woman vanished, melting into the shadows, as if they had been there solely to warn the gentleman that he had taken the wrong road. He wheeled around, circled the crucifix and galloped off along the other wider road until, beneath the bright sky, he caught sight of the black pillars and timbers of Hangman's Hill. He stopped and stood up in his stirrups. On a high, barren hill on which neither grass nor gorse grew, rose the four granite pillars, huge and black in the yellow moonlight, like the four corners of a ruined house, joined by a low, crumbling wall. On the top of the pillars were four thick beams and from the beams hung four hanged men, black and stiff in the still, silent air. Everything around them was as dead as they were.

Fat carrion birds were asleep perched on the timbers. Beyond, glittered the pale, dead waters of the Lake of Ladies and the moon rose round and full in the sky.

Don Ruy murmured the Lord's Prayer that every Christian owes to guilty souls, then he spurred his horse on and was about to pass by when he heard a voice ring out in the midst of that immense silence and solitude, a voice calling out to him in hesitant, pleading tones:

134

'Sir, stop, come here!'

Don Ruy pulled sharply on the reins and, standing up in his stirrups, gazed around with terrified eyes at the sinister landscape. All he could see was the bleak hill, the silent, glittering water, the timbers, the dead men. He thought it might have been an illusion brought on by the night, or some prank played on him by an errant demon. Then, calmly, untroubled and without haste, he spurred his horse on again as if he were riding down a street in Segovia. Behind him, though, the voice called out again, more urgently this time, anxious, almost anguished:

'Sir, wait, don't leave, turn round, come here!'

Again Don Ruy stopped, turned in his saddle and looked fearlessly at the four bodies hanging from the beams. That was where the voice had come from and, since it was a human voice, it could only come from a human form. It must therefore be one of the hanged men who had called out to him with such urgency and longing.

Could one of them, by some marvellous mercy of God, still have breath and life? Or could it be that by some even greater marvel, one of those half-rotten corpses was holding him back in order to give him some message from beyond? Regardless of whether the voice came from a living breast or a dead one, it would be an act of great cowardice to gallop off, terrified, without first listening and helping.

He rode his trembling horse back up the hill and then stopped, sitting calm and erect in the saddle, one hand on his hip. Looking hard at each of the four hanging bodies in turn, he cried out:

'Which of you hanged men dares call out to Don Ruy de Cárdenas?'

Then, as calmly and naturally as a man at his window chatting with someone in the street, the one with his back to the full moon spoke out from where he hung high up on the rope:

'Sir, it was I.'

Don Ruy urged his horse forwards. He could not make out the man's face which was sunk on his chest, hidden by his long, dark, dishevelled hair. He could only see that his hands hung loose and unfettered, as did his bare feet, already dried to the colour of bitumen.

'What do you want of me?'

The hanged man sighed and murmured:

'Sir, would you do me a great favour and cut this rope from which I hang.'

Don Ruy took out his sword and with one sure blow cut the half-rotten cord. With a sinister sound of rattling bones the body fell to the ground where it lay for a moment, outstretched. Almost at once, however, it stood up on numb, unsteady feet and raised a dead face to Don Ruy; it was a skull to which the skin still clung, yellower than the moonlight illuminating it. In his eyes there was neither movement nor light. His lips were fixed in a permanent grin. From between his white, white teeth emerged the tip of a very black tongue.

Don Ruy revealed neither terror nor disgust. Casually sheathing his sword he asked:

'Are you dead or alive?'

The man slowly shrugged his shoulders.

'I don't know, sir. Who knows what life is? Who knows what death is?'

'But what do you want of me?'

With his long, fleshless fingers the hanged man loosened the knot in the rope still encircling his neck and declared with great serenity and firmness:

'Sir, I am to accompany you as far as your destination, Cabril.'

Don Ruy shuddered and pulled so hard on the reins that his horse reared up as if it, too, were amazed.

'Come with me to Cabril?'

The man bent his back along which, through a long tear in his woollen shirt, you could see his vertebrae, sharper than the teeth of a saw.

'Sir', he begged, 'don't deny me this. For I will earn a great reward if I do you this great service.'

The thought crossed Don Ruy's mind that this could well be some terrible trick of the Devil's. Fixing his brilliant eyes on the dead face looking anxiously up at him, awaiting his consent, he very slowly and deliberately made the sign of the cross.

The hanged man bent his knees in startled reverence.

'Sir, why do you put me to the test with that sign? Only through the Cross can we find redemption and it is from the Cross alone that I seek mercy.'

Don Ruy decided that if this man had not been sent by the Devil, he might very well have been sent by God, and so, devoutly, with a humble gesture that indicated his submission to the will of Heaven, he nodded and accepted his terrifying companion:

'If you truly have been sent by God, then come with me to Cabril. But I will ask you nothing and you must ask me nothing.'

He rode back to the brilliant, moonlit path. The hanged man was still by his side, running with such light steps that he managed to keep up with Don Ruy even at a gallop, as if he were borne along by a silent wind. Sometimes, in order to breathe more freely, he loosened the knot of the rope hanging round his neck and when they passed by hedges that gave off the scent of wild flowers, the man would murmur with infinite relief and delight:

'How good it is to run again!'

Don Ruy was still in a state of mingled amazement and torment. He realised now that this was a body resuscitated by God in order to undertake some strange and secret mission. But why had God given him such a terrifying companion? To protect him? To prevent Doña Leonor, beloved by Heaven for her piety, from falling into mortal sin? Did the Lord have so few angels in Heaven that he was forced to employ a hanged man to perform such a divine errand of mercy? He would happily have ridden back to Segovia were it not for his gallant, gentlemanly sense of loyalty, his pride, which would not allow him to turn back, and his submission to the orders of God which he now felt weighing upon him.

When they reached a high point along the road, they suddenly saw Cabril below them, the towers of the Franciscan monastery gleaming white in the moonlight, the houses sleeping amongst the gardens. In absolute silence, with not one dog barking from behind the gates or walls, they rode down to the old Roman bridge. There, by the crucifix, the hanged man fell to his knees on the flagstones, raised the pale bones of his hands in prayer and remained there for a long time, sighing deeply. Then, when they reached the path, he drank long and gratefully from a fountain that flowed and sang beneath the branches of a willow. Since the path was very narrow, he walked ahead of Don Ruy, silent, hunched, his arms folded tightly across his chest.

The moon was high in the sky now. Don Ruy gazed with some bitterness at that full, lustrous disc shedding its brilliant, indiscreet light upon his secret. A night that should have been divine was being ruined: a huge moon was emerging from behind the hills to illuminate everything below and a hanged man had stepped down from the gallows to accompany him, apparently knowing everything about him. God had ordered it thus. Yet how sad to arrive at that sweet door, so sweetly promised, with such an intruder at his side and beneath that brilliant sky.

Suddenly the hanged man stopped, raising one arm from which the sleeve hung in shreds. They had reached the end of the path that opened out onto a broader, smoother road and before them stood the long, white wall surrounding Señor de Lara's garden. On it was built a mirador with stone verandas, all overgrown with ivy.

'Sir,' murmured the hanged man, placing his hands respectfully on Don Ruy's stirrup, 'just a few steps along from this mirador is a door through which you are to go into the garden. If you believe your horse to be sure and faithful, it would be best to leave him here tethered to a tree. On the enterprise upon which we are embarked, even the noise of our footsteps could prove too much.'

Silently, Don Ruy dismounted and tethered his horse, whom he knew to be faithful and sure, to the trunk of a withered poplar.

So submissive had he become to the commands of this

companion imposed on him by God that he followed after him without further ado, keeping close to the moonlit wall.

Slowly and cautiously, tiptoeing along in his bare feet, the hanged man went on ahead, keeping a sharp eye on the top of the wall and peering into the gloom of the shrubbery, stopping to listen to noises that he alone noticed, for Don Ruy had never known a night so locked in deep and silent slumbers.

Such a degree of fear in someone who should have been indifferent to human perils, in turn filled the brave knight with such intense caution that he unsheathed his dagger, wrapped his cloak about his arm and walked alertly on, eyes glinting, as if in expectation of an ambush or a fight. Thus they reached a low door which the hanged man pushed open and which turned on its hinges without so much as a creak. They walked down a pathway lined by thick yew trees until they reached a pond full of water lilies and surrounded by rough stone benches shaded by the branches of flowering trees.

'That way!' murmured the hanged man, holding out his withered arm.

Beyond the pond lay an avenue shaded by a vault of dense and ancient trees. They walked down it, like shadows among the shadows, the hanged man first, Don Ruy following lightly behind, not touching a branch, barely touching the ground. A tiny thread of water whispered amongst the grasses. Roses climbed about the trunks, exuding sweet perfumes. Don Ruy's heart began to beat again with hopes of love.

'Shh!' said the hanged man.

Don Ruy almost bumped into the sinister figure, who had come to an abrupt halt, his arms spread wide as the crossbeams on a gate. Ahead of them, four stone steps led up to a brightly lit terrace. Crouching down, they climbed the steps and, at the far end of a formal, treeless garden arranged in neat flowerbeds bordered by low box hedges, they saw one side of the house bathed in the full glare of the moonlight. In the middle, between the closed windows, was a stone balcony with pots of marjoram at each corner; the doors to this balcony stood wide open. The room within, which lay in darkness, looked like a black hole in the moonlit façade. Leaning against the balcony was a ladder with rungs made out of rope.

The hanged man dragged Don Ruy away from the steps back into the shadows of the avenue. There he explained in urgent, commanding tones:

'Sir! You must now give me your hat and your cloak. You must stay here in the shadow of these trees. I am going to climb up that ladder and look into the room. If everything is as you would desire, I will return to this spot and may you be at peace with God . . .'

Don Ruy recoiled in horror at the idea of that creature climbing up to the balcony. He stamped his foot and gave a strangled cry.

'By God, no, I won't let you do it!'

The hanged man's hand, however, livid in the darkness, had already whisked the hat from Don Ruy's head and the cloak from his arm and he was soon well covered and muffled up in them, murmuring, this time in an anxious, supplicating voice:

'Don't deny me this, sir, for if I do you this one great service, I will be shown great mercy.'

And with that, he bounded up the steps and stood on the broad, brilliantly lit terrace.

Don Ruy watched, stunned. It was a miracle! For that man was himself, Don Ruy, to the very life, the way he stood and the way he walked with proud, light steps past the flowerbeds and the low box hedges, one hand on his waist, his face raised smilingly up at the window, the long scarlet plume of his hat bobbing triumphantly. The man was bathed now in splendid moonlight. The room of love awaited him, black, its doors open. Don Ruy watched, his eyes glittering, trembling with amazement and rage. The man had reached the ladder. He pushed back his cloak and put his foot on the first rung – the wretched man was going up, roared Don Ruy to himself! The hanged man was going up the ladder. The tall figure which was himself, Don Ruy, was now half-way up the ladder, black against the white wall. He stopped. No, he did not stop, he continued on up, reached the top and rested one cautious knee on the edge of the veranda. Don Ruy was watching desperately with his eyes, his soul, with every inch of his being. Then, suddenly, a black shape rushed out of the black room, a furious voice cried: 'Villain, villain!' and the blade of a dagger glinted, fell and rose again, glinted and fell and rose again, and again plunged in. The hanged man fell from the top of the ladder and landed on the soft earth like a heavy bundle of clothes. The balcony doors immediately clattered shut, and there was nothing now but silence, a soft serenity, the moon hanging very high and round in the summer sky.

Don Ruy understood in a flash what the treacherous plot had been. He unsheathed his sword and withdrew into the darkness of the avenue; then – another miracle – he saw the hanged man come running back across the terrace. He seized Don Ruy's sleeve and cried to him:

'To horse, sir, and away you go, for your rendezvous tonight was not with love but with death!'

They both ran down the avenue, past the pond beneath its shelter of flowering bushes, along the narrow road edged with yew trees and through the gate where they stopped for a moment, panting, on the road where the moon, ever more brilliant, ever rounder, was shining bright as day.

Then, and only then, did Don Ruy discover that the hanged man still had a dagger plunged up to the hilt in his chest, the point emerging, clean and glittering, from between his ribs. But the terrified man was tugging at him, hurrying him on:

'To horse, sir, and away you go. We could yet be betrayed.'

Trembling, longing to put an end to an adventure so full of marvels and horrors, Don Ruy took up the reins and galloped furiously off. The hanged man immediately leaped onto the back of the faithful horse. The good gentleman shuddered to feel that corpse behind him, a corpse that had been hanged on the gallows, then pierced by a dagger. With what desperation, then, did he gallop down that endless road. Despite the furious gallop, the hanged man never moved, he sat rigidly on the back of the horse, like a bronze statue on a pedestal, and all the time Don Ruy felt a bitter cold freezing his back, as if he were carrying a sack full of ice. When they passed the stone cross he murmured: 'Save me, Lord!' Beyond the stone cross, he was suddenly filled by the terrifying, fanciful thought that this grim companion might remain with him for ever and it would be his destiny to gallop through the world, in eternal night, with a dead man at his back. Unable to contain himself, he shouted behind him into the wind that beat about them as they fled:

'Where do you want me to take you?'

The hanged man, holding so tightly to Don Ruy that the latter could feel the hilt of the dagger sticking into him, whispered:

'Sir, would you be so kind as to leave me on Hangman's Hill.'

This gave sweet and infinite relief to the good gentleman for the hill was already near, he could see it now in the pale moonlight, with its pillars and its black beams. The horse came to a halt, trembling and flecked with foam.

Then the hanged man slid noiselessly down from the horse's back and, like a good servant, held Don Ruy's stirrup for him. His head raised, his black tongue poking out further between his white teeth, he muttered one last respectful plea:

'Sir, would you do me the great service of hanging me once more from my gallows.'

Don Ruy shivered with horror:

'Good God! You want me to hang you?'

The man sighed, opening wide his long arms:

'Sir, it is the will of God and the will of She who is even dearer than God!'

Resigned, submissive to these orders from above, Don Ruy dismounted and began to follow the man who walked thoughtfully over to the hill, his spine bent, the spine from which emerged the sharp, glinting point of the dagger. They both stopped beneath the empty gallows. The other corpses still hung from their gallows. The silence was sadder and deeper than other earthly silences. The water in the lake had grown black. The moon was sinking and fading.

Don Ruy looked at the beam from which hung the short piece of rope that he had cut off with his sword.

'How can I hang you?' he explained. 'I can't reach that

piece of rope with my hand and I can't possibly lift you up there on my own.'

'Sir,' replied the man, 'there's a long coil of rope in a corner somewhere here. You tie one end of it to the knot around my neck, the other end you throw over the beam and then pull, you're strong enough, and that way you can hang me.'

Stooped and with slow steps, they both searched for the coil of rope, and it was the hanged man who found it and unravelled it. Don Ruy took off his gloves. On the other man's instructions (he had learned his lesson well from the hangman) he tied one end of the rope to the knot the man still had around his neck and threw the other end, which snaked through the air and over the beam, so that it hung down to the ground. Then the strong, young gentleman, digging in his heels and bracing his arms, hoisted the man up until he hung there, swaying black in the air, one more hanged man amongst the others.

'Are you all right like that?'

The dead man's voice came back, hesitant and faint:

'Sir, I am as I should be.'

To hold him there, Don Ruy wrapped the rope several times round the stone pillar. Taking off his hat, wiping away the sweat drenching his brow with the back of his hand, he regarded his sinister and miraculous companion. He hung as stiffly as he had before, his face obscured by his dishevelled hair, his feet rigid, polished and worm-eaten as an old carcass. The dagger remained plunged in his chest. Above him, two crows were sleeping peacefully.

'Do you have any further requests?' asked Don Ruy, putting on his gloves again.

Faintly, from on high, the hanged man murmured:

'Sir, I would be most grateful if, when you reach Segovia, you would give a faithful account of this to Our Lady of the Pillar, your patroness, from whom I expect great mercies for my soul, for the service which, on her orders, my body performed for you!'

Don Ruy de Cárdenas understood everything when he heard that and, kneeling down devoutly at that place of pain and death, he said a long prayer for that worthy hanged man.

Then he galloped back to Segovia. Morning was breaking as he rode in through the San Mauros Gate. In the clear air, the bright bells were ringing out for matins. Still dirty and dishevelled from his terrible journey, Don Ruy went into the Church of Our Lady of the Pillar, threw himself down before the altar and confessed to his divine patroness the vile reason that had taken him to Cabril, told her of the help he had received from Heaven and, with hot tears of repentance and gratitude, swore to her that he would never again desire what was sinful nor allow worldly, evil thoughts into his heart.

4

In Cabril at that precise moment, Don Alonso de Lara, his eyes bulging with shock and fear, was scouring his garden, every path, every corner, every bit of shade.

At daybreak, after listening at the door of the bedroom where Doña Leonor had spent the night, he had gone quietly down to the garden and, failing to find the body of Don Ruy de Cárdenas beneath the balcony, at the foot of the ladder, as he had gleefully expected he would, he had convinced himself that the hated man must still have had some life in him when he fell and have dragged himself off, bleeding and moaning, in an attempt to reach his horse and to flee Cabril. With a dagger still plunged in his chest – a dagger Don Alonso had stabbed him with three times – the villain would barely have been able to drag himself more than a few yards and he must therefore be lying in some corner nearby, cold and stiff. Don Alonso then searched every path, every scrap of shade, every clump of bushes and, miracle of miracles, he found no body, no footprints, no churned-up earth, not even a drop of blood. And yet, with greedy, certain hand, he had plunged the dagger three times into the man's chest and left the dagger buried there.

The man he had killed was Don Ruy de Cárdenas, whom he had recognised at once from the dim depths of the room where he had lain in wait, as he crossed the brilliant, moonlit terrace, trusting, jaunty, one hand on his hip, his face smilingly lifted and the feather on his hat bobbing triumphantly. How could such a thing happen? How could a mortal body survive being pierced three times by a blade that had remained plunged in its heart? And the strangest thing was that Don Ruy's strong body had left not a trace on the ground beneath the veranda, in the bed of wallflowers and lilies, despite falling so heavily and from such a height, like a heavy bundle of clothes.

Not one flower was crushed, they all stood there like new, erect and fresh, with tiny drops of dew upon them. Frozen with a fear that bordered on terror, Don Alonso de Lara stood there, considering the balcony, measuring the height of the ladder, gazing in confusion at the bright wallflowers upright on their stems with not a stalk or a leaf bent. He began running wildly about the terrace and up and down the avenues and paths lined with yew trees, still hoping to find a footprint, a broken branch, a single blood stain on the fine sand.

Nothing! The whole garden seemed unusually neat and tidy, as if untouched even by the defoliating wind or the drying sun.

Still consumed by doubt and confusion as evening fell, he took a horse and left for Segovia with neither servant nor stable boy. Stooped and furtive as if he were some fugitive from the law, he entered his palace by the garden door and the first thing he did was run to the vaulted gallery, unbolt the shutters and peer avidly out at Don Ruy de Cárdenas' house. All the windows of the archdeacon's former home were in darkness, wide open, breathing in the cool of the night, and a stable lad was sitting at the door on a stone bench, lazily tuning his guitar.

Deathly pale, Don Alonso de Lara went down to his room; clearly no misfortune could have occurred in a house where all the windows stood open to the night air and where servants sat at their leisure at the street door. Then he clapped his hands and shouted angrily for his supper. No sooner had he sat down at the head of the table, on his tall chair of tooled leather, than he called in his manservant to whom, with unaccustomed familiarity, he immediately offered a glass of good wine. The man stood by his side respectfully sipping the proffered wine, while Don Alonso, tugging at his own beard and forcing a smile onto his sombre face, asked for the latest news or gossip in Segovia. During the days he had been absent in Cabril, had no event provoked fearful murmurings in the city? The servant dabbed at his lips and said that nothing had happened in Segovia that had caused any such talk, apart from the fact that Señor Don Gutierres' daughter, so young and so rich, had taken the veil in the Convent of the Discalced Carmelites. Don Alonso insisted, fixing his servant with voracious eyes. Had there been no great duel? Had no young gentleman, well-known in Segovia, been found badly wounded along the road to Cabril? The servant shrugged. He had heard nothing in the city of duels or wounded gentlemen. With an irritated wave of his hand, Don Alonso dismissed the servant.

He dined but frugally and then returned to the gallery to peer out at Don Ruy's windows. They were closed now; in the last window on the corner, he could see a flickering light. Don Alonso watched all night, tirelessly going over and over in his mind the same fearful question. How had that man escaped with a dagger through his heart? How was it possible? When morning broke, he put on a cloak and a large hat and went down to the courtyard, carefully muffled up, his face covered, and waited near Don Ruy's house. The bells rang for matins. Merchants, their jackets still unbuttoned, came out to raise the shutters on their shops and to hang up their signs. Vegetable sellers cried their wares, spurring on donkeys laden with baskets, and barefoot friars, a satchel over one shoulder, begged for alms and blessed the young girls who passed by.

Pious women carrying heavy black rosaries, their faces hidden by large hoods, filed eagerly into the church. Then the towncrier, pausing on one corner of the courtyard, blew a horn and began reading out a proclamation in a booming voice.

Señor de Lara stood for a moment by the fountain as if absorbed in the music of the water flowing from the three fountain spouts. It suddenly occurred to him that the proclamation being read out by the towncrier might perhaps mention Don Ruy's disappearance. He ran to the corner of the courtyard, but the man was already rolling up his scroll of parchment and moving majestically off, thumping the flagstones with his white stick as he went. And when Don Alonso looked back at the house, his astonished eyes fell on Don Ruy, the same Don Ruy whom he had killed, making his jaunty, elegant way to church, his smiling face lifted to the cool morning air; he was wearing a pale jacket, with matching feathers in his hat, one hand at his waist, the other distractedly brandishing a cane decorated with golden tassels and fringes.

Don Alonso returned to his house with the doddering footsteps of an old man. At the top of the stone steps he met his old chaplain, who had come to greet him and who, going with him into the antechamber, first asked reverently for news of Doña Leonor and then told him of an extraordinary incident that had been the cause of much speculation and fear throughout the city. The previous evening, when the Mayor went to visit Hangman's Hill – for the festival of the Holy Apostles was fast approaching – he discovered, to his great shock and horror, that one of the hanged men had a dagger plunged in his chest. Was this a joke on the part of some sinister prankster, some act of vengeance that not even death could assuage? Even odder was the fact that the body had evidently been taken down from the gallows and dragged through a garden (for they had found young green leaves caught up amongst the old rags) and then hanged again with a new rope. These were turbulent times indeed when not even dead men could escape such outrages.

Don Alonso listened, his hands trembling, his hair standing on end. He fell immediately into a state of anxious agitation, shouting and bumping into doors; he wanted to go at once to see this grim act of profanation with his own eyes. Taking two hastily saddled mules he set off for Hangman's Hill, dragging the astonished chaplain with him. A lot of people from Segovia had gathered on the hill, gazing in amazement at the grotesque horror of the scene: a hanged man killed and hanged again. They all drew back when they saw the noble Señor de Lara hurrying towards them up the hill. Dazed and deathly pale, he looked at the hanged man and at the dagger piercing his chest. It was his dagger; he had killed the dead man!

He fled at once back to Cabril to shut himself away with his secret, and there he languished, grew wan and pale, avoiding all contact with Doña Leonor, skulking along the dark, shady paths of the garden, mumbling words into the wind, until on the morning of St John's day, a maidservant on her way back from the fountain with her bucket found him dead beneath the stone balcony, stretched out on the ground, his fingers clawing at the earth in the bed of wallflowers where, it seemed, he had spent a long time scrabbling in the soil, looking for something . . .

5

In order to flee these painful memories, Doña Leonor, heiress to all the wealth of the Lara estate, withdrew to her palace in Segovia. Now, however, knowing that Don Ruy de Cárdenas had miraculously escaped the ambush in Cabril, and spending each morning peering out from between the half-open shutters, following his every move with tireless eyes that grew damp with tears as he strolled across the courtyard to the church, she chose not to visit the church of Our Lady of the Pillar as long as she remained in deep mourning, fearful of her own impetuous, impatient heart. Then, on the first Sunday morning when she could don purple silks instead of black crepe, she went down the steps of her palace, walked across the flagstones of the courtyard and through the doors of the church, her face pale with a new and precious emotion. Don Ruy de Cárdenas was kneeling before the altar where he had placed his votive bouquet of yellow and white carnations. When he heard the rustle of fine silks, he looked up, his eyes as full of pure, celestial hope as if an angel had called him. Doña Leonor knelt down, her breast heaving, very pale and very happy, paler than the wax tapers, happier than the swallows flying freely about the arches of the old church.

Before that same altar, kneeling on those same flagstones, they were married by Don Martinho, the Bishop of Segovia, in the autumn of the Year of our Lord 1475, when Isabel and Ferdinand reigned over Castile, those strong, Catholic monarchs through whom God performed great deeds on both land and sea.

JOSÉ MATIAS

Lovely afternoon, my friend! . . . I'm here for José Matias'
funeral – José Matias d'Albuquerque, the Visconde de
Garmilde's nephew. I'm sure you knew him: he was slim
and blond as an ear of corn, with the curled moustaches of
a knight-errant and the hesitant mouth of a contemplative.
He was a clever chap with a kind of refined, sober elegance.
He had an enquiring mind too . . . very keen on general ideas
in logic and with a penetrating enough wit to understand
my *Defence of Hegelian Philosophy*! But that image of José
Matias dates from 1865. The very last time I saw him was
one bitter January evening and he was sheltering in a doorway in Rua de São Bento, shivering with cold in a pale
brown jacket out at the elbows, and stinking horribly of
brandy.

    That's right, you dined with him once at the Paço do
Conde! He'd stopped off in Coimbra on his way back from
Oporto. And Craveiro – who at the time was engaged in
writing *The Ironies and Sufferings of Satan* in the hope of
further inflaming the quarrel between the Purists and the
Satanists – even recited that glumly idealistic sonnet of his that
begins: 'In the cage of my breast, my heart . . .' I can see José
Matias now, his satin cravat plump and black against his white
linen waistcoat, his eyes fixed on the candles in the cande-
labra, smiling wanly at that heart roaring inside its cage. It
was an April night and the moon was full. We all went for a
stroll afterwards across the bridge and through the Choupal
woods. A couple of us had our guitars with us and Januário
gave ardent voice to some of the sad, romantic songs of the
time:

Yesterday evening at sunset,
lost in contemplation and silent,
you gazed down at the mighty torrent
that lay boiling at your feet . . .

And José Matias stood leaning on the parapet of the bridge, looking soulfully up at the moon! Why not go with this interesting young man to the Cemitério dos Prazeres? I have a cab, a hired one, as befits a teacher of philosophy. What? You're worried because you're wearing light-coloured trousers! Oh, really, my friend! Of all the physical manifestations of sympathy, black cashmere is the most grossly material. Besides, the man we're going to bury was possessed of great spirituality.

Look, they're just bringing the coffin out of the church. Only three carriages to accompany him to the grave. The truth is, my friend, that the real José Matias, in all his brilliance, died six years ago. The half-decomposed remains being borne away in this box adorned with yellow are the remains of a drunkard with no history and no name, who died in a doorway, killed by the February frosts.

The man with the gold-rimmed glasses, in the coupé? I don't know, my friend. Some rich relative possibly, the sort who only turn up at funerals, with their relationship correctly draped in mourning, once the dead man can no longer demand anything of them or otherwise prove an embarrassment. The obese gentleman in the victoria, with the fat, yellow face, is Alves Capão. He owns a newspaper called *The Joke* in which philosophy, alas, plays little part. What was his relationship to José Matias? I don't know. Perhaps they got drunk in the same bars; perhaps latterly José Matias had become a contributor to *The Joke*; perhaps beneath all that fat and his appalling taste in literature, both equally repellent, there beats a compassionate heart. Here's our cab now . . . Shall I wind the window down? A cigarette perhaps? I have matches. José Matias was a disconcerting figure for someone like myself, who expects life to evolve logically and the corn to spring untrammelled from the seed. In Coimbra

154

we considered him to have a soul of almost scandalous banality, a judgement due perhaps in part to his depressingly immaculate appearance. His gown was never torn, there was never a speck of careless dust on his shoes, never a hair on his head or his moustache out of place in defiance of that rigid perfection. Furthermore, he was the only intellectual of our passionate generation who did not bemoan the ills of Poland, the only one who could read Hugo's *Les Contemplations* without turning pale or bursting into tears and remain unmoved by Garibaldi's many wounds! And yet there was nothing hard or cold or selfish or unfriendly about José Matias. On the contrary, he was a delightful companion, always good-humoured and ready with a gentle smile. His unshakeable serenity appeared to have its roots in an immense superficiality of feeling and, at the time, it seemed neither surprising nor inappropriate that we should nickname that softest, blondest, most lightweight of young men José Matias the Squirrelheart. His father had already died, followed soon afterwards by his mother, a lovely, courteous lady from whom José inherited fifty *contos*. So, when he graduated, José Matias went to live in Lisbon, to ease the solitude of his adoring uncle, General Visconde de Garmilde. I'm sure you remember him. He was the very image of the traditional general, with his great waxed moustaches, his pink military trousers pulled taut by the straps that went over his gleaming boots and, of course, the whip clamped beneath one arm, its point all a-quiver, as if aching to give the world a good hiding! He cut a grotesquely war-like figure, but he had a heart of gold. At the time, Garmilde lived in Arroios, in an old house decorated with tiles that had a garden where he showed himself to be an avid cultivator of magnificent dahlias. The garden sloped very gently up to the ivy-clad wall that separated it from another very large and beautiful rose garden belonging to State Counsellor Matos Miranda, whose house, with its elegant terrace set between two small yellow towers, was built on the top of the hill and was known as the Casa da Parreira, the house of the vine trellis. You'll have heard (at least by reputation, the way one has heard of Helen of Troy or Inés de Castro) of the lovely

Elisa Miranda, Elisa of the Casa da Parreira. Towards the end of the so-called Regeneration period, she was considered Lisbon's great romantic beauty, although, in fact, Lisbon only ever glimpsed her through the windows of her fine calèche or amongst the dust and the crowds of the city park when they hung up coloured lights in the trees there or at the two balls given at the Assembleia do Carmo, of which Matos Miranda was the honoured director. Whether out of some provincial taste for staying at home or because she belonged to that peculiarly serious bourgeois class which, in the Lisbon of the time, still kept up the old, severely reclusive customs or because of some paternalistic stricture imposed on her by her husband – already sixty years old and diabetic to boot – the Goddess rarely descended from Arroios to reveal herself to us mere mortals. But the one person who did see her constantly, indeed almost unavoidably once he'd moved to Lisbon, was José Matias. For the General's villa lay at the foot of the hill, below the Casa da Parreira and its garden, and the divine Elisa could not appear at a window, cross the terrace or pluck a rose from among the avenues of boxtrees without being deliciously visible and there were no trees in either of the two sunny gardens to extend a curtain of dense foliage between them. You have doubtless crooned, as we all have at some time, those hackneyed but immortal words:

It was autumn when I saw you, your face so bright, standing in the pale moonlight . . .

For poor José Matias' first glimpse of Elisa Miranda occurred in exactly those circumstances: one night on the terrace in the moonlight on his return from the beach at Ericeira in October, in the autumn. You never had the chance to gaze upon that Lamartinian beauty. She was tall, slender and supple, worthy of that comparison in the Bible with a palmtree in the wind. She had thick, glossy, black hair which she wore in a mass of ringlets about her temples. Her skin was the colour of fresh camellias! She had dark, liquid eyes, sad and languid, with long eyelashes . . . Ah, my friend, even I (at the time I was

156

writing my painstaking commentary on Hegel), even I, after seeing her one rainy afternoon as she waited for her carriage outside Seixas, adored her for three whole thrilling days and composed a sonnet in her honour! I don't know if José Matias wrote her sonnets, but all of us, all his friends that is, noticed at once the strong, deep, absolute love that was born in the moonlight that autumn night in a heart which, in Coimbra, we had considered to be a mere squirrel's heart.

It's understandable that such a quiet and cautious man would not go in for public displays of emotion. However, even in the time of Aristotle, it was said that there are two things that cannot be hidden: love and smoke. And love began to seep out of our impenetrable friend José Matias, like thin smoke through the invisible cracks in a locked house engulfed by flames. I remember visiting him once in Arroios on my way back from the Alentejo. It was a Sunday in July. He was going out to dine that night with a great-aunt, Dona Mafalda Noronha, who lived in Benfica at the Quinta dos Cedros, where Matos Miranda and the divine Elisa also dined every Sunday. I believe that house was the only place in which she and José Matias ever met, at least it was the only place that provided them with the necessary pensive avenues and quiet, shady nooks to do so. José Matias' bedroom windows opened out on to both his and the Mirandas' garden and when I entered his room that evening, he was still slowly getting dressed. Never, my friend, have I seen a human face bathed in a look of such sure, serene happiness! When he embraced me, he was smiling radiantly, a smile that came from the depths of an equally radiant soul. He smiled delightedly all through my account of the misfortunes that had befallen me in the Alentejo and, when I'd finished, he simply smiled ecstatically, commented on the heat and absent-mindedly rolled himself a cigarette. He wore the same absorbed smile as, with near religious scruple, he selected a white silk tie from a drawer. And irresistibly, out of a habit now as unconscious as blinking, his smiling eyes, full of a calm tenderness, kept returning to the closed windows. When I followed that happy gaze, I saw the divine Elisa, wearing a pale dress and a white hat, strolling lazily up and down the terrace of the Casa da Parreira, thoughtfully drawing on her gloves and glancing up at my friend's bedroom windows that glittered like gold in the oblique sun. Meanwhile, José Matias continued to talk, or rather mumble, about various pleasant subjects, never once losing his perennial smile. All his attention was concentrated on the mirror, on the coral and pearl pin for his tie, on the white waistcoat, which he buttoned and adjusted with the devotion of a young priest putting on his stole and amice to approach the altar, in the innocent exaltation of taking his first Mass. I have never seen a man splash eau de Cologne onto a handerkchief with such profound joy. And, after putting on his frock coat and placing in its lapel a single, superb rose, he solemnly flung the windows wide, with ineffable emotion, with a delicious sigh. *Introibo ad altarem Dei*! I remained discreetly slumped on the sofa. And believe it or not, my friend, I envied that man standing motionless and erect at the window in that state of sublime adoration, with his eyes and his soul and his whole being fixed on the terrace, on the white woman drawing on her pale gloves, and as indifferent to the world as if it consisted only of the stones she stepped on!

This state of joy, my friend, lasted for ten years and remained unvaryingly splendid, pure, distant and ethereal. Don't laugh . . . They certainly met at Dona Mafalda's house. They wrote to each other, voluminously, tossing the letters over the wall that separated the two gardens, but they never sought the rare delight of a stolen conversation over the ivy of that wall or the still more exquisite delight of a shared silence hidden in the shadows. And they never exchanged a kiss. I mean it! The occasional fleeting, passionate squeeze of a hand beneath the trees in Dona Mafalda's garden was all that was allowed within the exalted limits their wills imposed upon their desire. You probably can't understand how for ten long years two fragile bodies could withstand such a terrible, morbid state of renunciation . . . Of course, they had little opportunity to lose their honour, no time when they could be safely alone, no small gate in the dividing wall. For the divine Elisa really did live in a convent, whose bolts and bars were the rigidly reclusive habits of the gloomy diabetic Matos Miranda. But there was much moral nobility and subtle feeling in the chasteness of that love. Love makes a man more spiritual and a woman more material. Such spiritualization came easily to José Matias, who (without our suspecting it) had been born extravagantly spiritual; but the very human Elisa also found a delicate pleasure in that ideal monk-like adoration which, with its tremulous fingers entwined about a rosary, does not even dare to touch the tunic of the sublime Virgin. He loved it, of course. He discovered a kind of superhuman delight in that transcendentally dematerialized love. And for ten years, like Victor Hugo's Ruy Blas, he walked, fervent and bedazzled, through his own radiant dream, a dream in which Elisa actually lived inside his soul, in a fusion so absolute she became consubstantial with his own being! Can you believe that after discovering one evening in Dona Mafalda's garden that his cigarette smoke bothered Elisa, he actually gave up smoking, even when out riding alone through the outskirts of Lisbon?

The very real presence of that divine creature in his own being created in José Matias strange, new behaviour patterns that all grew out of that hallucinatory experience. For example, since the Visconde de Garmilde kept to the traditions of old Portugal and had supper early, José Matias dined after going to the Teatro São Carlos, in the delightfully nostalgic Café Central, where the sole seemed to have been fried in heaven and the wine to have been bottled there. He never dined without a profusion of candles and flowers on the table. Why? Because Elisa was his invisible companion at supper there. That was what lay behind all those silences bathed in a smile of religious intensity. Why? Because he was always listening to her. I remember how he removed from his room three classical engravings of lascivious fauns and swooning nymphs. The spirit of Elisa hovered in the atmosphere and so he purified the walls and ordered them to be lined with pale silks. Love, especially such an elegantly idealistic love, always proves expensive and José Matias was splendidly lavish with the luxuries he shared with her. He could not decently ride with the image of Elisa inside him in a hired carriage or allow her august image to touch the wicker seats in the stalls at the opera. He rode, therefore, in carriages that were simple and sombre in taste and he hired a box at the opera house where he installed, just for her, an armchair worthy of a pope, which he had upholstered in white satin embroidered with golden stars.

Furthermore, when he learned of Elisa's generosity, he at once became equally generous and on an equally sumptuous scale. No one else living in Lisbon at the time handed out one hundred-*mil-réis* notes with more ease or with a lighter heart. He had soon squandered sixty *contos* on the love of a woman to whom he had never even given a flower!

And what was Matos Miranda doing all this time? The good man neither spoiled the perfection nor disturbed the tranquillity of that happiness! Was José Matias' spirituality so absolute that he was genuinely interested only in Elisa's soul, indifferent to the acts submitted to by that base, mortal shell, her body? I don't know, but it would be safe to say that the grave and worthy diabetic, always muffled up in a dark woollen scarf, with his grizzled side whiskers and heavy gold-rimmed spectacles, certainly never evoked any disquieting images of husbandly ardour, an ardour that would inevitably, albeit involuntarily, have ignited an answering spark in his wife. Even I, a philosopher, could never understand the almost affectionate concern shown by José Matias for the man whom right and custom allowed (however indifferently) to watch Elisa unlacing her white petticoat! Was it in recognition of the fact that it was Miranda who had first chanced upon the divine woman in some remote Setúbal street (where José Matias would never have discovered her), who had kept her in comfort, well-nourished and finely dressed and provided her with only the best-sprung carriages? Or had she whispered to José Matias that well-worn promise: 'I'm neither yours, nor his', which, because it so flatters the ego, makes up for all the sacrifice? I really don't know. But one thing is sure, his magnanimous disdain for Miranda's physical presence in the temple wherein dwelt his Goddess gave a perfect unity to José Matias' happiness, like a pure crystal unscratched

160

and unblemished that sparkles with equal brilliance from whichever angle you view it. And that happiness, my friend, lasted for ten whole years. An outrageous luxury for a mere mortal!

But one day, the earth trembled beneath José Matias' feet, an earthquake of unparalleled horror. In January or February of 1871, Miranda, his health already undermined by diabetes, died of pneumonia. I dawdled along these same streets in another hired carriage behind *his* funeral procession, a lavish affair packed with government ministers, for Miranda was very much part of the Establishment. Afterwards, I made use of the same carriage to visit José Matias in Arroios, not out of morbid curiosity nor in order to proffer any unseemly words of congratulation, but so that he should have the moderating force of philosophy beside him at that crucial moment. I found him, however, in the company of an old and trusted friend, the brilliant Nicolau da Barca, whom I have since also driven to this cemetery beneath whose stones lie all those comrades with whom I once built castles in the air . . . Nicolau had arrived early that morning from Velosa, from his villa in Santarém, summoned there by a telegram from José Matias. When I got there, a servant was busy packing two enormous suitcases. José Matias was leaving for Oporto that night. He was even ready and dressed in a travelling suit, all in black apart from his yellow leather shoes. He shook me by the hand and then, while Nicolau was mixing us a hot toddy, he kept pacing about the room in a kind of stunned silence, with a look that was neither excitement nor modestly disguised joy, nor even surprise at the sudden transformation of his fortunes. No, if Darwin's book *The Expression of the Emotions in Man and Animals* is right, the only emotion apparent in José Matias that afternoon was embarrassment! Across the way, in the Casa da Parreira, all the windows were tight shut against the sadness of the grey afternoon. I even caught José Matias casting a quick glance at the terrace, a glance that revealed disquiet, anxiety, almost terror! How can I can put it? It was the kind of anxious glance you'd give a restless lioness locked up in only the flimsiest of cages. When he went into his bedroom for a moment, I muttered to Nicolau over our hot toddies: 'Matias is absolutely right to go to Oporto.' Nicolau shrugged: 'Yes, he thought it would be the decent thing to do, and I agreed. But only, of course, for the months of deepest mourning.' At seven o'clock we accompanied our friend to Santa Apolónia station. On the way back, with the rain beating hard on the carriage roof, we mused upon the subject. I smiled contentedly: 'A year of mourning and then lots of happiness and lots of children. It's a perfect poem!' Nicolau added more seriously: 'A poem written in the most delicious and succulent prose. The divine Elisa gets to keep both her divine status and Miranda's fortune, some ten or twelve *contos* a year. For the very first time in our lives, you and I are witnesses to an example of virtue rewarded!'

But, my friend, the months of strict mourning came to an end and several more months went by, without José Matias showing any sign of leaving Oporto. I found him that August ensconced in the Hotel Francfort, where he passed the melancholy of the scorching noonday heat smoking (for he had taken it up again), reading Jules Verne novels and drinking iced beer until the evening grew cool. Then he would get dressed, dab on some eau de Cologne and put a flower in his buttonhole in preparation for supper at São João de Foz.

But despite the blessed approach of an end to the mourning period and to all that desperate waiting, I saw no hint in José Matias of any elegantly repressed tumult, or impatience with the slow passage of time, which so often moves with the deliberate, stumbling gait of an old man. On the contrary, the smile of radiant certainty that in recent years had lit up his face with a glow of perfect bliss had been replaced by a look of heavy seriousness, all shadows and furrowed brows, the look of someone struggling with some ever-present, nagging doubt, painful and insoluble. Shall I tell you what I think? All that summer, in the Hotel Francfort, it seemed to me that every moment of his waking life, whether he was down-ing a cool glass of beer or pulling on his gloves before getting into the carriage to go out to supper, José Matias was constantly

162

and anxiously asking his conscience: 'What should I do? What should I do?' And later, one day at lunch, he said something that really surprised me. He opened the newspaper and exclaimed, with a rush of blood to his cheeks: 'What! You mean it's the 29th of August already? Good grief! Nearly the end of August!'

I returned to Lisbon. The winter passed, very dry and blue. I was working on my *Origins of Utilitarianism*. One Sunday, in the Rossio, when there were already carnations on sale outside the tobacconists' shops, I spied the divine Elisa, with purple feathers in her hat, going by in a carriage. And that same week, in my copy of the *Diário Ilustrado*, I found a brief, almost timid announcement of the marriage of Senhora Dona Elisa Miranda. And to whom do you think, my friend? Why, to the well-known landowner, Senhor Francisco Torres Nogueira!

(My friend made a fist and thumped his thigh in amazement.) At the time, I too raised both my fists to Heaven, where all earthly actions are judged, and I screamed out my fury at the falseness, the slippery, treacherous inconstancy, the deceiving turpitude of women in general and of Elisa in particular, cursed among all women. To betray the noble, pure, intellectual José Matias and his ten years of sublime, submissive love so hastily, so precipitately, when she was barely out of mourning!

And, having raised my fists to Heaven, I then clutched them to my head, crying: 'But why, why?' Could it have been for love? For years she had loved that young man with a love that knew neither disillusion nor satiety since it remained in suspension, immaterial and unsatisfied. Could it have been out of ambition? Like José Matias, Torres Nogueira was a pleasant idler and owned, in mortgaged vineyards, the same fifty or sixty *contos* that José Matias had just inherited from his Uncle Garmilde in the form of excellent, debt-free lands. So why? Doubtless because Torres Nogueira's great black moustaches made a stronger appeal to her flesh than José Matias' hesitant, blond down! Ah, how right St John Chrysostom was when he taught that woman is but a heap of ordure piled at the gates of Hell!

Then one afternoon, when I was still raging to myself in the same vein, I met our friend Nicolau da Barca in Rua do Alecrim. He leaped from his carriage, pushed me into a doorway, my poor arm in his excited grasp, and blurted out: 'Have you heard? It was José Matias who turned her down. She wrote to him, went to Oporto, wept . . . He wouldn't even see her! He didn't want to get married, he *doesn't* want to get married!' I was stunned: 'But then she . . .' 'Hurt and under siege by Torres, weary of widowhood and still a beautiful thirty-year-old in the first bloom of life, what could the poor woman do but get married!' I raised both arms to the arched roof of the doorway in which we were standing: 'But what about José Matias' sublime love?' Nicolau, his close friend and confidant, replied with utter certainty: 'It remains unchanged: infinite and absolute. But he doesn't want to marry!' We looked at each other, then parted, shrugging our shoulders with the resigned astonishment that befits prudent spirits confronted by the Unknowable. But, being a philosopher and therefore an imprudent spirit, I spent the whole night dissecting José Matias' actions with the blade of a psychology specially honed for the purpose. By dawn I was utterly exhausted and could only conclude, as one always concludes in philosophy, that I was faced with a First Cause, by its very nature impenetrable and on which the point of my instrument would instantly break, affording no advantage to him, to me or to the World.

So the divine Elisa got married and continued living at the Casa da Parreira with Torres Nogueira, in the peace and comfort she had once enjoyed with Matos Miranda. Towards midsummer, José Matias left Oporto for Arroios and his Uncle Garmilde's mansion, where he moved back into his old rooms with the balcony looking onto the garden, full of now untended dahlias. August arrived, hot and silent, as it always does in Lisbon. On Sundays, José Matias dined with Dona Mafalda de Noronha in Benfica, alone – for, unlike Matos Miranda, Torres Nogueira was not acquainted with that venerable lady from the Quinta dos Cedros. In the evenings, the divine Elisa in her pale dresses walked in the garden amongst the roses. So the only change, in that sweet corner of Arroios, seemed to be the fact that Matos Miranda lay in his beautiful marble tomb in the Cemitério dos Prazeres and Torres Nogueira lay in Elisa's excellent bed.

However, another change, an immense and painful one, had also taken place – the change in José Matias! Can you imagine how that poor unfortunate spent his sterile days? With his eyes, memory, soul, indeed his whole being, fixed on the terrace, the windows, the gardens of the Casa da Parreira. But he no longer watched with the windows flung wide, in open ecstasy, wearing a smile of assured beatitude. He hid behind closed curtains, peering through a tiny crack, stealing furtive glimpses of the white folds of her white dress, his face devastated by pain and defeat. And can you understand why that poor heart suffered so? Presumably because Elisa, rebuffed by his unwelcoming arms, had run immediately, without a struggle, without scruples, into other more accessible and willing arms. No, my friend, that was not the case! Consider now the complex and subtle nature of this passion. José Matias remained devoutly convinced that, in the depths of her soul, in the sacred spiritual depths untouched by social convention, the decisions of pure reason, the impulses of pride or the desires of the flesh, Elisa loved him and only him, with a love that had not perished or changed, which, even though it remained untended and unwatered, continued in exuberant bloom like the ancient Mystical Rose.

What tortured him, my friend, what carved deep lines in his face in the space of only a few short months, was that a man, a male, a brute should have possessed the woman whom he considered his, that a man (in the most holy and socially acceptable way, beneath the tender patronage of Church and State) should, to his heart's content, sully with his stiff, black moustaches the divine lips that Matias (too filled by the superstitious reverence, indeed almost terror, that he felt for Elisa's divinity) had never dared to brush with his. What can I say? The feelings of this extraordinary fellow José Matias were like the feelings of a monk who, prostrated in transcendental ecstasy before an image of the Virgin, is rudely interrupted by

165

a gross sacrilegist, who climbs up onto the altar and obscenely lifts the Virgin's skirts. You smile . . . But what about Matos Miranda? Ah, my friend, he was diabetic, serious and fat and was already installed in the Casa da Parreira, together with his obesity and his diabetes, long before José first met Elisa and gave her both life and heart for ever. But this Torres Nogueira with his black moustaches and his fleshy arms, this man, who had so brutally smashed his way through this purest of pure loves with the vigour and drive one would expect of a former catcher of bulls, had simply swooped down and carried the woman off and may even have taught her what it meant to have a real man as a husband!

But, for heaven's sake, she was the woman he'd rejected when she'd offered herself up to him with all the freshness and generosity of a love that scorn had not yet withered or cast down. What did he expect? But that was the nature of José Matias' extraordinarily tortuous spirituality. After a few months he had forgotten, genuinely forgotten, his insulting rejection of her, as if it had been a slight misunderstanding over some financial or social matter, something that had happened months before in the North, something whose reality and slightly bitter aftertaste distance and time had mitigated. And now, here in Lisbon, with Elisa's windows facing his and the perfumes of the roses in their two gardens mingling in the shadows, the cause of his present pain, his real pain, was that he had loved a woman sublimely and had placed her up among the stars in order to adore her still more purely, only to have some dark brute with black moustaches snatch the woman from among the stars and hurl her into bed!

A complicated case, eh? In my role as philosopher, I philosophized long and hard about it and I concluded that José Matias was a sick man with a bad attack of hyperspirituality – a virulent, putrid inflammation of the spirit – who had a horror of the material aspects of marriage: the slippers, the touch of clammy morning skin, the six long months of enormous swelling belly, the children screaming in their wet beds . . . And now he cried out in fury and torment because a certain outright materialist next door had been prepared to accept Elisa, woollen nightdress and all. Was he some kind of imbecile? No, my friend, merely an ultraromantic, crazily indifferent to the potent realities of life, who could never imagine that slippers and dirty nappies are things of great beauty in a house filled by sunlight and love.

And do you know what further exacerbated his torment? It was the fact that Elisa showed herself to be as much in love with him as ever. What do you think? Ghastly, eh? Or rather, whilst she may not have felt the strong, unique love, completely unchanged in its essence, that she had once felt, she did still feel an irresistible pull towards poor José Matias and she constantly repeated the gestures of that former love. Perhaps it was just the chance circumstance of their gardens being next door to each other. I don't know. But from September onwards, when Torres Nogueira left for his vineyards in Carcavelos to supervise the grape harvest, she took up her position on the edge of the terrace, looking out across the roses and dahlias in full bloom, and began again that sweet transmission of sweet looks with which for ten years she had enraptured José Matias' heart.

I don't think they passed notes to each other over the garden wall as they had under the paternal regime of Matos Miranda. Even from afar, from amongst the vineyards of Carcavelos, the new master of the house, the strong man with the black moustaches, imposed a mood of reserve and prudence on the divine Elisa. Calmed by the presence of her strong, young husband, she would feel less need for discreet encounters in the tepid shade of night, even supposing that her moral elegance and José Matias' rigid idealism would have allowed them to make use of a ladder placed against the garden wall. Besides, Elisa was fundamentally honest and she retained a more sacred respect for her body, which she perceived as having been beautifully and carefully fashioned by God, than for her soul. And who knows? Perhaps the adorable woman belonged to the same magnificent race as that Italian marchioness, Giulia di Malfieri, who kept two lovers at her service, a poet to tend her romantic sensibilities and a coachman for her baser needs.

But, my friend, let us delve no further into the psychology of this living woman as we follow after the man who died for her! The fact is that, almost without realizing it, Elisa and her friend fell back into that old idealized union enacted across the flowering gardens. And in October, since Torres Nogueira was still away at the wine harvest in Carcavelos, José Matias joyfully opened his windows wide again in order to contemplate the terrace of the Casa da Parreira.

You would think that in recovering the idealism of his former love, such an exaggeratedly spiritual man would also regain his former state of perfect happiness. He reigned supreme in Elisa's immortal soul, what did it matter if another possessed her mortal body? But no, the poor man suffered terrible anguish and to shake off the pain of these torments, he, who had always been so serene and mildmannered, was seized by a terrible restlessness. His life, my friend, became a whirlwind, a maelstrom! For a whole year, while still in the grip of despair, his behaviour left Lisbon society troubled, shocked and stunned. Some of his more legendary extravagances date from that period. Have you heard, for example, about the supper he held? He invited thirty or forty of the stupidest, filthiest women he could find in the dark backstreets of the Bairro Alto and the Mouraria. He then ordered them to clamber onto donkeys, while he mounted a large, white horse and rode at their head, wielding a huge whip, and led them in grave, melancholy procession all the way up to Graça to greet the rising sun!

But all this commotion did nothing to dissipate his pain and it was then, that winter, that he took to gambling and drinking. He would shut himself up in his house all day and sit with his eyes and soul fixed (from behind closed windows now, for Torres Nogueira had returned from the vineyards) on that fateful terrace. Later, at night, when the lights in Elisa's windows went out, he would sally forth in an old carriage (he always used the same one, Gago's) to play roulette at Bravo's, then on to Club Cavalheiro, where he would gamble frenetically until it was time for a late supper in a private room in some restaurant, lit by clusters of burning candles, with wine, champagne and cognac in full, desperate flow.

And that Fury-driven life lasted for years, for seven years in all. He drank and gambled away the lands his Uncle Garmilde had bequeathed him and was left only with the big house in Arroios and the ready cash he had obtained from mortgaging it. Then suddenly he disappeared from all the bars and gambling dens. And we learned that Torres Nogueira was dying of dropsy.

Around that time, because of a deal involving Nicolau da Barca (a complicated matter, something to do with a bill of exchange), who had telegraphed me anxiously from his villa in Santarém, I went to visit José Matias in Arroios at ten o'clock one warm April night. Leading me along the badly lit corridor, stripped now of the sumptuous chests and carvings from India that had belonged to old General Garmilde, the servant confessed to me that his master had not yet finished dinner. It still makes me shudder to remember the desolate impression poor José made on me. He was in the room that opens onto the two gardens. In front of a window, concealed by the damask curtains, was the gleaming table on which stood two candlesticks, a basket of white roses and some of Garmilde's splendid silver. To one side, José Matias lay slumped in an armchair, apparently either asleep or dead, his white waistcoat unbuttoned, an empty glass in one inert hand, his pale face sunk onto his chest.

When I touched him on the shoulder, he looked up with a start, his hair all dishevelled, and said: 'What time is it?' In order to rouse him, I cried out gaily that it was late, ten o'clock already, and he at once filled his glass from the nearest bottle of white wine and drank it down slowly, his hand trembling terribly. Then, pushing back his hair from his clammy forehead, he said: 'So, what's new?' With staring eyes, he listened uncomprehendingly, as if in a dream, to the message Nicolau had sent him. At last, with a sigh, he stirred a bottle of champagne in its ice bucket, filled another glass and murmured: 'It's so hot! I'm so thirsty!' But he didn't drink, instead he hauled his heavy body up out of the wicker armchair and staggered over to the window where he threw back the curtains and then flung wide the windows. He stood there unmoving, as if surprised by the silence and the dark solace of the starry night. I peered out too. In the Casa da Parreira shone two brightly lit windows, open to the soft breeze. And against that brilliant light, on the edge of the terrace, stood a pale figure wrapped in the long folds of a white robe, seemingly lost in thought. It was Elisa. Beyond her, in the bright room, her husband no doubt lay gasping for breath, his lungs horribly congested. She was standing utterly still, sending her sweet gaze, perhaps even a smile, to her sweet friend. Fascinated, the poor unfortunate man held his breath and drank in the delights of that beneficent vision while, between them, in the soft night, all the flowers of their two gardens exhaled their perfumes. Then suddenly, Elisa went back in, drawn away by a moan or some impatient word uttered by Torres Nogueira. The windows were closed and all light and life vanished from the house.

José Matias gave a heartrending sob, overflowing with pain, and stumbled so badly that he had to grab one of the curtains for support, tearing it as he did so. He then fell helpless into the arms I held out to him and I dragged him to his chair, as if he were a corpse or a drunk. But to my amazement, after only a moment, that extraordinary man opened his eyes, smiled a slow, blank smile and murmured almost serenely: 'It's the heat . . . It's so hot! Are you sure you wouldn't like some tea?'

I declined and fled, whilst he, indifferent to my flight, stretched out again in the armchair and, with unsteady hand, lit a huge cigar.

Good heavens, we're in Rua Santa Isabel already! These brutes are certainly in a hurry to consign poor José Matias to dust and the final worm. Anyway, soon after that curious night, Torres Nogueira died. During that new period of mourning, the divine Elisa withdrew to the villa of a sister-in-law who was also a widow and lived in the Villa Côrte Moreira, near Beja. And José Matias disappeared completely, he simply vanished into thin air. No news or even rumours about him reached me, especially once the mutual friend through whom I might expect to receive word, the brilliant Nicolau da Barca, in fulfilment of the traditional, almost social duty of the consumptive, had left for the island of Madeira with what remained of his lungs but with no real hope of recovery.

I spent that whole year immersed in writing my *Essay on Affective Phenomena*. Then, one day, at the beginning of summer, I was walking down Rua de São Bento, looking for no. 214 where Morgado d'Azemel's library was in the process of being catalogued, when who should I see on the balcony of a new house on the corner but the divine Elisa, feeding lettuce leaves through the bars to a caged canary. And she looked lovely, my friend, fuller and mellower, a mature woman now, soft and desirable, despite having celebrated her forty-second birthday in Beja! But then, that woman belonged to the same race as Helen, who even forty years after the siege of Troy, could still dazzle both mortal men and the immortal gods. And, oddly enough, later that afternoon I learned the latest episode in the life of that admirable Helen from João Seco, the librarian in charge of cataloguing the Morgado library.

The divine Elisa now had a lover. And this was simply because she could not, with her usual honesty, take him as her third lawful husband. The lucky man whom she adored was in fact married. He had married a Spanish woman in Beja but, after a year of marriage and various affairs on the side, she had left for Seville to celebrate Holy Week and ended up in the arms of a wealthy cattle breeder. Her placid husband, a supervisor in the Ministry of Public Works, remained in Beja, where he was also vaguely involved in teaching some vague kind of drawing. Now one of his students was the daughter of the owner of Villa Côrte Moreira and it was in that garden, whilst he guided the little girl's pencil, that Elisa met him and fell in love with such an urgent passion that she snatched him away from the Ministry of Public Works and dragged him off to Lisbon, a city better suited than Beja to the enjoyment of a scandalous and secret happiness. João Seco is also from Beja and had spent Christmas there. He knew the supervisor and the ladies from Villa Côrte Moreira and he understood the whole story at a glance when he looked out one day from the

171

windows of no. 214, where he was cataloguing the Morgado library, and saw Elisa on the balcony on the corner and the ex-supervisor slipping happily in through the street door, well-dressed, well-shod, in pale gloves, and looking infinitely happier to be engaged in those private works than he had ever looked in performing his duties at the Ministry of Public Works.

And I, too, saw the ex-supervisor for the first time from that same window at no. 214. He was a good-looking, well-built chap, with a pale complexion and a dark beard, who fulfilled all the conditions as regards quantity (and perhaps even quality) necessary to fill a widowed and therefore (as the Bible would have it) empty heart. I was a frequent visitor to no. 214 because I was interested in the catalogue of that particular library, for Morgado d'Azemel, thanks to the random ironies of various legacies, possessed an incomparable collection of works by eighteenth-century philosophers. Some weeks went by and then one night as I was leaving (for João Seco worked at night), I stopped by an open doorway further along the street to light a cigar and, in the tremulous glare of the match, I saw José Matias standing in the shadows. But what a José Matias, my friend! To get a better look, I struck another match. Poor man! He had allowed his beard to grow, a strange beard, hesitant and scrubby, with the texture of yellowing cotton wool. He had let his hair grow too. It hung in dry, stringy strands from beneath a battered derby, but everything else about him seemed diminished and shrunken inside a crumpled double-breasted jacket of cheap wool and a pair of black trousers with deep pockets into which his hands were plunged in the infinitely sad but age-old gesture of the idle poor. Gripped by a mixture of astonishment and pity, I could only stammer out: 'Hello, what are you doing here? What's up?' And, in a voice coarsened by brandy, he replied with his usual gentle courtesy, albeit rather abruptly in an attempt to disguise his embarrassment: 'I'm waiting for someone.' I didn't press him. I walked on but looked back to verify what a sudden flash of intuition had told me. The dark doorway stood immediately opposite the new building and Elisa's balcony.

172

José Matias lived hidden in that doorway for three years!

It was one of those doorways-cum-hallways you often find in the old part of Lisbon. Perennially dirty, with no porter's lodge, they stand with their doors always gaping wide, like caves built along the side of the street, from which no one bothers to expel those in hiding there from poverty or pain. To one side there was a tavern. As night fell, José Matias would walk down Rua de São Bento, keeping close to the wall and then merging like a shadow into the shadows of the doorway. By that time, the lights would be on in Elisa's windows. In winter they would be blurred by the fine mist and in summer they would remain open to the calm, quiet air. José Matias would stand before them, his hands in his pockets, deep in contemplation. Every half hour, he would slip surreptitiously into the tavern. A glass of wine, a glass of brandy and then, discreetly, he would slip back into the darkness of the doorway, into his ecstatic trance. When the lights in Elisa's windows went out, even through the long night, even through the dark, winter nights, he would stay there, hunched, transfixed, stamping his worn soles on the flagstones, or sitting inside, on the steps of the staircase, his dull eyes fixed on the black façade of the house where he knew she would be sleeping with the other man.

At first, in order to smoke a snatched cigarette, he would climb up to the deserted landing to conceal the flame that might betray his hiding place. But later, he took to smoking incessantly, leaning against the doorframe, pulling anxiously on his cigarette so that the tip would glow and light up his face. And do you know why, my friend? Because Elisa had discovered that there in that doorway, looking up in submissive adoration at her windows, as soulfully as ever, was her poor José Matias.

And would you believe it, every night from then on, either from behind the glass of the windows or leaning on the balcony (the ex-supervisor would be inside reading the evening paper, reclining on the sofa with his slippers on), she would stand very still and gaze down at the doorway, her face expressionless but sending out the same wordless gaze she had always sent him from the terrace, over the roses and the dahlias. Astonished, José Matias understood and desperately tried to keep his cigarette glowing, like a lighthouse, to guide her beloved eyes in the dark and show her that he was there, all hers, transfixed and ever faithful.

He never walked down the Rua de São Bento by day. He wouldn't have dared to in his jacket out at the elbows and his worn boots. For that young man, who had once dressed with such fine, sober elegance, had fallen into ragged poverty. Where he got the few coins every day to buy his wine and a serving of salt cod in the taverns, I don't know. But may the divine Elisa be praised, my friend! With great delicacy, by clever and devious means, she, the wealthy woman, managed to set up a pension for José Matias, the beggar. A piquant situation, eh? The grateful lady bestowing two monthly allowances on her two men – her physical lover and her spiritual lover. He, however, guessed the origin of that terrifying charity and refused it, politely, humbly, even tenderly, even with a tear in those eyes now inflamed by brandy!

Only at dead of night did he dare to walk down Rua de São Bento and slip into his doorway. And how do you think he spent the rest of the day? He spent it spying on that ex-supervisor for the Ministry of Public Works, following him and trailing him. Yes, my friend, he felt an insatiable, frenetic, terrible curiosity about the man whom Elisa had chosen. Her two previous husbands, Miranda and Nogueira, had entered Elisa's bedroom publicly, via the Church, and for human ends other than love – to have a home, possibly children, stability and a quiet life. But this man was simply her lover, whom she had chosen and kept purely in order to be loved, and the only rational motivation behind their relationship was the union of their two bodies. He never wearied, therefore, of studying him, his physique, his clothes, his manners, anxious to discover what the man was really like, this man whom Elisa had preferred above all others to be her other half. For decency's sake, the supervisor lived at the other end of Rua de São Bento, opposite the market. And it was there, where Elisa's eyes could not see him and his ragged state, that José Matias went early each morning to observe and follow the man when, still warm from her cosy bedroom, he left Elisa's house. From that moment on he never let him out of his sight. He would follow him furtively, from a distance, like a pickpocket. And I suspect that he did so less out of perverse curiosity than to ensure that, despite all the temptations of Lisbon, overwhelming for a public works supervisor from Beja, the man kept himself pure for Elisa. He kept an eye on the lover of the woman he loved in the interests of preserving her happiness.

What extreme refinement of spirituality and devotion, my friend! Elisa's soul was his and the perennial recipient of his perennial adoration. And now he wanted Elisa's body to be no less faithfully adored by the man to whom she had given it. But it was easy for the ex-supervisor to be faithful to such a lovely and wealthy woman, with her silk stockings and diamond earrings, who quite simply dazzled him. And who knows, my friend, perhaps this faithfulness, this carnal reverence for Elisa's divinity, was the last happiness life bestowed on José Matias. The reason I think this is because, one rainy morning last winter, I came across the ex-supervisor buying camellias in a florist's in Rua do Ouro and on the other side of the road, on the corner, the gaunt, tattered figure of José Matias was watching him affectionately, almost gratefully. And perhaps that night, shivering in his doorway, stamping his drenched feet, and with his eyes, soft with tenderness, fixed on the dark windows, he would have thought: 'Poor love, poor Elisa! She must have been so pleased with the flowers he bought her!'

This went on for three years.

Finally, the day before yesterday, João Seco turned up at my house in the evening and told me breathlessly: 'They've taken José Matias off on a stretcher to the hospital, with congestion of the lungs!'

It seems they found him at dawn, lying on the pavement, all hunched up in his thin overcoat, gasping for breath. His face, wearing a deathlike pallor, was still turned towards Elisa's balcony. I raced to the hospital but he was already dead when

I got there. I went up to the infirmary with the doctor on duty. I lifted the sheet that covered him. In the opening of his torn and dirty shirt, tied round his neck by a cord, was a small silk pouch, equally covered in dust and dirt. It doubtless contained a flower, a lock of hair or a scrap of lace belonging to Elisa, dating from those first magical days, those evenings in Benfica. I asked the doctor, who knew and pitied him, if he had suffered at all: 'No, he was in a coma for a while, then he opened his eyes very wide and exclaimed "Oh!" as if terribly surprised, and that was that.'

Was it his soul crying out in amazement and horror at finding that it too must die? Or was it the soul triumphant, recognizing that it was at last immortal and free? It's not for us to know. Even the divine Plato didn't know and nor will the last philosopher on the very last evening of the world.

Ah, here's the cemetery. I think we should stick close by the coffin. It's very odd to see someone like Alves Capão paying his sad respects to our poor spiritual friend. But good Lord, look! There, waiting, at the door of the church, that serious-looking man in tails and a grey overcoat. It's the supervisor from the Ministry of Public Works and he's carrying a huge bunch of violets. Elisa has sent her physical lover to accompany her spiritual lover to the grave and to cover him with flowers. But, my friend, let us only hope that she would never have asked José Matias to scatter violets on the supervisor's corpse! For whilst Matter may not understand Spirit, or necessarily draw upon the Spirit for its own happiness, it will neverless always do obeisance to the Spirit and will always treat itself, even in the midst of its own pleasure, with brutality and disdain. That supervisor with his bunch of flowers must be a great consolation to a metaphysician who, like me, wrote commentaries on Spinoza and Mallebranche, rehabilitated Fichte, and proved beyond doubt the illusion of sensation! For that reason alone it was worth accompanying this unexplained man, José Matias, to his grave, for he was perhaps more than just a man, or then again, perhaps less. Yes, you're right, it is cold . . . Still, it's a lovely afternoon!

The Maias – *Eça de Queiroz*

Margaret Jull Costa's translation of *The Maias* won the PEN/
Book-of-the-Month-Club Translation Prize for 2008 and
the Oxford Weidenfeld Translation Prize for 2008.

'Eça de Queiroz spent eight years writing *The Maias*. This is a
novel in the tradition of Flaubert or Dickens, in which de
Queiroz anatomizes a society through a brilliant drama of a
family's decline and downfall. Margaret Jull Costa's translation
is supple, transparent and wonderfully paced. There seems to
be no barrier at all between the reader and what the author
intended. The novel shades from realism to romanticism, from
satire to tragedy. The vigour and charm of the characters
come across beautifully in this translation, and so does de
Queiroz's biting, sometimes despairing view of Lisbon society
in the last quarter of the nineteenth century.'
> *Helen Dunmore, novelist and chair of the Oxford*
> *Weidenfeld Translation Prize*

'Over the years Margaret Jull Costa has produced a number of
notable translations of the fiction of Eça de Queiroz, the great
Portuguese novelist, who is widely considered to be one of
the major European novelists of the 19th century, often
ranked with Flaubert, Balzac, Dickens, and Tolstoy. Most
recently, Margaret Jull Costa turned her hand to *Os Maias*,
Eça de Queiroz's greatest work, and the results are stunning.
The sensuous elegance of the prose vividly captures the greatness of the original, bringing the novel to life for the reader in
a way only the most masterful of translations can do. Clearly a
labor of love, Margaret Jull Costa's brilliant translation of *The
Maias* stands as a masterpiece in its own right. Eça de Queiroz
lives in English!'
> *The Judges of the PEN/Book-of-the-Month-Club*
> *Translation Prize*

'José Maria de Eça de Queiroz occupies the same sort of place
in Portuguese Literature as Dickens does in English, Balzac
does in French and Tolstoy does in Russian. *The Maias*,
first published in 1888, is not just the story of a fictional
family over 70 years or a panoramic sweep across 19th-century

Portugal, but a powerful portrait of a society in inexorable moral decline. Its blend of romanticism and realism is a magnificent achievement, revealed in all its glory in this brilliant new translation by Margaret Jull Costa.'

Keith Richmond in Tribune

'A veteran translator of Saramago and Pessoa, Jull Costa delivers Queiroz's 1888 masterpiece in a beautiful English version that will become the standard. Rich scion Carlos de Maia – like his best friend, writer João da Ega – is an incorrigible dabbler caught in the enervated Lisbon of the 1870s. His parentage is checkered: Carlos's mother runs off with an Italian, taking his sister, Maria, but leaving Carlos with his father, Pedro, who soon shoots himself. Raised by Pedro's father, Afonso, the adult Carlos returns with a medical degree to live with Afonso in the family's cursed Lisbon compound. His very romantic, very doomed affair with Madame Maria Eduarda Gomes sets in motion a train of coincidences, deftly prefigured, that resonantly entwines Carlos's fate with that of his father and spreads all of Portuguese society before the reader. Queiroz has a magisterial sense of social stratification, family and the way Eros can make an opera of private life. The novel crystallizes the larger unreality of an incestuous society, one that drifts, even the elite heatedly acknowledge, into decline. The neglect of the big Iberian 19th-century novelists – Galdós, Clarín and Queiroz – remains a puzzle. This novel stands with the great achievements of fiction.'

Publishers Weekly* starred review

'Eça is the master of the narrative finale, usually accomplished through dialogue linked to skilfully deployed symbolism. The last scene of *The Maias*, in which Carlos and Ega, having agreed on the ultimate futility of effort in their lives, suddenly race to catch a tram, offers a fine flourish of comic irony. Margaret Jull Costa's new English version expertly captures the novelist's refined amalgam of the acerbic satirist and compassionate observer.'

Jonathan Keates in the Times Literary Supplement

£15.00   ISBN 978 1 903517 53 6   714p   B. Format

The Crime of Father Amaro – *Eça de Queiroz*

'A major source of pleasure and one of its many strengths is its wide-ranging panoply of perspectives, its generosity in assigning chapters to be fleshed out by the lesser characters and its depiction of their idiosyncrasies: the pious and easily offended pharmacist Carlos; the gluttonous Libaninho with his penchant for rice puddings and port; and the lazy, sleezy Canon Dias, Amaro's superior, who becomes a gloating accessory to his crimes. The use of suspense and ellipsis ensures the narrative is compelling; its plot at times almost takes a turn into Gothic territory. Margaret Jull Costa provides a solid, clear and flowing translation, which ensures that Eça's drily understated satire, his harsh but lucid critique of human selfishness and inadequacy are telling; it also reflects his engaging sense of bathos and all that is amusingly grotesque.'

> *Daniel Lukes in The Times Literary Supplement*

'*The Crime of Father Amaro* is also the best possible introduction to Portuguese literature. It is the first great realistic novel in the language; a product of the wonderful period when it seemed to be easy, all over Europe, to write novels of the highest literary quality which were also commercial successes. So it is instantly approachable, while at the same time complex and ultimately mysterious. All these riches are made available in a brand new translation. When *The Crime of Father Amaro* was first translated, very inadequately, in the sixties, it still made quite a stir, but was quickly forgotten. Dedalus deserve every credit for promoting Eça once again. Margaret Jull Costa's new translation is far better than the earlier one. She translates everything, for one thing (the sixties version is full of omissions). She shows considerable skill and tact in handling the tricky problems posed by Portuguese names, of people and of places, and by the technical vocabulary of the Church. These things, the curse of poor translators, are treated simply and naturally without the need for footnotes. The rich patterning of the text survives as a deeply satisfying experience.'

> *Tom Earle in The London Magazine*

£11.99   ISBN I 873982 89 5   476p   B. Format

The Tragedy of the Street of Flowers- *Eça de Queiroz*

'Attractive and repellent by turns, Genoveva is a splendid creation who almost achieves stature and sympathy sufficient for tragedy in a novel otherwise suffused with irony and bathos. Through her, Eça anatomises Portuguese society, cutting through its superficial elegance to the inadequacy and insecurity he discerns – with sympathy – underneath. *The Tragedy of the Street of Flowers* justifies his claim to be numbered among the great European novelists of his day.'
Paul Duguid in The Times Literary Supplement

'One of the greatest novelists of the novel's greatest age, Eça is also amongst the most readable due to his narrative energy, sweeping range and tart sense of humour.'
Michael Kerrigan in The Scotsman

'Narrative pace, fluency and ruthless satire characterises Queiroz's writings. The most frequent object of his satire is the decadence of the bourgeoisie and aristocracy in late 19th-century Lisbon – with all its attendant misery and sacrifice. The protagonists are typical of Queiroz's work: the fat libertine who buys his pleasure; the English governess, a stick with more desires than Venus; the maid of a thousand lovers; the aspirant painter who changes his aesthetic more often than his socks; the Anglophile uncle, full of decency, understanding and beliefs cast in iron; the law graduate who aspires to the sentimental and the poetic and whose masterpiece is finally published in a woman's magazine; a high class prostitute with the bearing of royalty. The pressing logic of the plot, the clarity and occasional lyricism of the prose, as well as the mastery of dialogue, make Queiroz a formidable author, so it is more surprising that translations of his books in English are so rare. Huge praise, then, to the publishers for their determination to make available major works that are otherwise neglected in Anglophone countries, and to the translator, Margaret Jull Costa, whose achievement is giving the impression that Queiroz might have written the English himself.'
Henry Sheen in The New Statesman

£9.99   ISBN 978 1 873982 64 8   346p   B. Format